Promise to Love Me

Promise to Love Me

MAUREEN WOODS

To order additional copies of this book, contact:
Xlibris Corporation
1-888-795-4274
www.Xlibris.com
Orders@Xlibris.com
46780

PREFACE

I WOULD LIKE to think that this novel is the gateway to a future that one could only dream about. Dreams are just those until you find the courage to turn them into reality. Writing is something I have always loved, and this novel is an investment of many long, tiring hours and months of commitment and determination.

What I have come to learn is that the style of writing articulates the author, meaning there is no right or wrong way to how we express ourselves. It is our own uniqueness and distinction that we share with our readers that allows them to define who we really are.

I have to dedicate this novel to a very dear friend of mine who was a deep inspiration and there for me every step of the way. His faith in me was tremendous, and he made me realize I had a gift that should not be hidden.

Keith, this one is for you! Thank you so much for believing in me and staying by my side through it all. You were my rock and such a great friend. Also, to my parents, Carl and Bonnie, and my three precious children, Ryan, Tyler, and Paige, who mean everything to me.

I would like to share with you a quote that I once came across.

"A friend is someone who knows the song in your heart and can sing it back to you when you have forgotten the words."

REFLECTIONS

Looking in the large oval mirror

Silvered and spotted with time

Wondering just who it is that I see

A mirror image of someone I am

Reflections of time gone past

Impressions of truth

Ironic and depicting of self

No illusions or mirage of distortion

My hands making contact with the glass

Fingers moving over its flawlessness

Careful not to break the perfection

That so loosely hangs on the wall

The symbolization of me

Realistic and feeling with no substitution

For who I am on the outside

– Maureen Woods

CHAPTER 1

ALTHOUGH THE WEATHER was normal for this time of year, the rain pouring down had attitude and temperament as Amy trudged along shivering. Visibility was near impossible, and all she could count on was putting one foot in front of the other and keep going. Although there were no gusts of wind, soggy leaves lay about, letting off a stinky odor, while the landscape lay in stark contrast to the beauty that normally drew the eye in the warmer season. Everything looked so plain and dismal, which could leave the most jubilant person feeling gloomy. Lawns turned into minilakes, and the streets flowed with murky water badly in need of drainage. Unsightly was what it was. "Good golly, this is horrible." Coming to a stop, she eased herself onto a bench along the side of the road and waited for a bus. Being able to sit, she was grateful for as her feet were sore, and she was beyond exhausted. The weight of the water on her body was a heavy burden, and she felt like a drowned rat. The bench, she noticed, was in great need of repair, for it lacked sturdiness, and the paint was peeling. Rickety is how she would describe it. As her cold fingers fumbled with the heavy wet cuff of her coat, a passing vehicle sent a spray of water in her direction. "Idiot . . . inconsiderate idiot." Wiping the moisture from her watch, she checked the time. Not long now and the bus should be along. She was thankful for the lack of traffic along this somewhat busy road. With tears stinging her eyes, she rested her head on the back of the bench, wishing she had something in her purse to help get rid of the pounding headache. The coffee she held in her hand did nothing to ward off the chill that racked her body as it was no longer hot. "Damn," she muttered under her breath. Allowing the rain to hit her face, she let out a sigh. Being separated and having to go out into the world for the first time to find work was not as easy as it seemed, but she just had to do it. There was no choice. It wasn't that there was just herself to think about; there was also her twelve-year-old daughter. Here she was out in this lousy weather catching her death. At the moment, she would gladly welcome it, if it came. Maybe if she just closed her eyes. Her day couldn't possibly get any worse than it was. Absorbed in thought, Amy did not hear the bus pull up. "Hey, lady, you wanting on?" Slowly getting up, the water running down her coat in one big slosh, Amy tossed her cup into the garbage bin and boarded the bus. Looking about, the aisle had the appearance of needing a good mopping, and the air had a smell of mustiness about it. The driver looked at her with sympathy. "Hope you weren't waiting long, miss, as it's a wet one today." With lack of a smile, Amy nodded. "Sure is." Although it was crowded at this time of day with most people just getting off work, she managed to find an empty seat to herself. Talking to anyone right now was furthest from her mind. Not that she was an unfriendly sort, but was just not up for any conversation. She had a hell of a day and was still jobless, even though she walked the walk and talked the talk. It really wasn't a question of "if" she could find work, it was "when." She certainly wasn't looking forward to doing this all again tomorrow or the next day. The state she was now in was not worth it, or so she told herself. It was luck that she needed. Just pure, plain, simple luck. "Right. *Luck.* That has never been a positive word in my course of life, although I guess there is a first for everything," she mumbled under her breath. As the bus pulled away from the curb, Amy removed her hat, brushing aside the soaked strands of brown hair from her face and leaning against the foggy window, listening to the sound of the window wipers as they moved back and forth. *Swoosh swoosh, swoosh swoosh.* The creaking sound that they made did nothing to calm her mood, except make her clench her fist in frustration. She was at the limit, nervewise. Life held no satisfaction, and she had lost that glow awhile back. The air from the heater blew the top of her hair, and it was such warmth to her body that she did not move. She welcomed it. Her thoughts drifted to Paula, her daughter, who she knew would have a hug waiting when she heard the sound of the front door opening. The two of them always prepared dinner together, and Amy was proud of her developing culinary skills. Amy let out a little smile at the thought of her bouncing around the kitchen and full of nonstop chatter, with her long brown hair tied back in ponytails. Unknowingly, she kept her world together and was the only good thing in her life and made home what it was. Home. At one time it meant a husband, a dog, and a huge fenced yard. Now it meant just her and Paula in a tiny two-bedroom townhouse with very little yard for either of them to enjoy. Lifting her head, she focused her eyes on a woman with two children in tow, hurrying along to their destination. *You poor things*, she thought. As the bus came to a halt, Amy realized it was time to get off. Although the ride had not been a long one, she was glad for the solitude. As the doors opened, she stepped off, adjusted her coat, and put on her hat. The rain was still coming down hard, sounding like the intense beating of a drum. Taking a deep breath, she knew she did not have that far of a distance to walk; but as weary as she was, it seemed like miles to go. Just as she moved from where she had been standing, a man came toward her in great haste, signaling for the almost – departing bus to wait. Before either of them realized it, their paths collided, knocking the wind out of her. Losing her balance, Amy landed in a puddle and could feel the water soaking through her thin slacks. Cursing as she tried to stand up, she felt a hand on her arm.

"I am very sorry, ma'am. Allow me to help you." Supported back onto her feet, Amy was just on the verge of telling this man exactly what she thought of him, when she directed her eyes to his. Looking into the bluest eyes she had ever seen, Amy was fixated until the man before her emitted a wicked grin as if he understood the kind of impression he had on females. Realizing what she had been doing and feeling slightly embarrassed, Amy decided to just turn around, head home, and put the whole incident out of her mind. She took her first step when he caught her arm, whirled her around, and kissed her. Releasing her, Amy stepped backward and wiped her hand across her lips while glaring at him.

"Why y-you . . ." And before he knew what was happening, her hand made contact with his cheek. Narrowing his eyes, he touched the affected area.

"Do you always make it a habit of slapping men when you first meet them?"

Amy was shaking like a leaf, not sure if it was due to feeling the cold or her jussive mood. The expression on her face was one of utter despair and rage. "Only the clumsy ones that upend me into a puddle because they don't watch where they're going. Then you violate my person by . . . by . . . *kissing me*. Of all the nerve!"

Finding this all very amusing, he laughed. "I see. Well, allow me to introduce myself, and I hope it will not earn me any more of your insults. My name is Aaron."

Ignoring the introduction, she stood there without saying a word. As far as she was concerned, she did not care to know the name of this rogue or be in his presence much longer.

"So the lady does not have a name?"

"Perhaps, but *not* that you need to know it. What makes you think I would want to stand here and befriend you anyways. What did you say your name was? *Arrogant?*"

Taking a step forward, he took hold of her wrist. "Why, you little –"

"You have no right to touch me, and if you don't remove your hands this instant, I will scream."

"I bet you've got a good set of lungs to go with that big mouth of yours," Aaron said between clenched teeth.

"Ooooh." Amy took the heel of her boot and stomped on his foot. "You are the most uncouth male that I have ever encountered."

"And you are the most infuriating female that I have ever met. Most ill-tempered too."

"Maybe if you were to shut your mouth and open your eyes, you'd see the state you left me in. Thanks to you, I am drenched to the skin. The last thing I want to be doing is st-standing out in this miserable weather any longer. It hasn't been that much of a pleasant experience, I can assure you. So unless you are desperately in need of human feeling, you'll allow me to be on my way, and I hope to never bump into you again."

Chuckling, Aaron folded his arms and looked at her. "If you remember correctly, I was the one who bumped into you."

"Whatever. Let me paraphrase then. I hope to never see the likes of you again. Did you understand *that?*" As she turned around to leave, he seized hold of her. "What now?"

"You're not leaving before telling me your name. This has really been a rather harmless situation, don't you think?"

"What I think is . . . is that you're a cad, and the word *no* is obviously not in your vocabulary." With a self-satisfied smile on his face that Amy had the urge to wipe off, Aaron lifted his hand and tilted her chin slightly upward. "Matter of fact, I cannot say it is a word that I am familiar with, love."

"I am not your *love*, so please don't call me that."

Aaron laughed at the fire smoldering in her eyes, and what a vision she was. "Well now, since I don't know your name, that was the best I could come up with."

She knew she had been had. Looking at Aaron with nothing but irritation, she mumbled under her breath. "If that is the only way I will be rid of you . . . Amy. My name is Amy."

"Pretty name for such a delightful lady. It is nice to meet you." Holding out his right hand, it was a moment before he finally let it drop back down to his side untouched. "Could I interest you in a coffee at all? There is a cafe just around the corner, and it is the least I can do."

"Thanks, but no thanks, and you have done quite enough already, I might add. My day has been a very long one, and in case you haven't noticed, I'm dripping wet. I wouldn't be the least bit surprised if I am catching a cold this very minute. I need to get home and out of these clothes, so . . . so good-bye." Amy turned and started walking up the sidewalk when she heard footsteps following closely behind.

"Allow me to accompany you since coffee is out of the question."

Stopping, she peered at him. "I live close by, and I don't need an escort, *thank you very much*." As Amy carried on without interruption, Aaron lit a cigarette and strolled behind just to get a sense on her course of direction. It wasn't long before he saw her turn into a set of townhouses, so striding away, he hailed a cab that was coming his way. "Where to, sir?"

Putting out his cigarette, he opened the door and slid into the backseat. "Two hundred fifty-six Harlow Street."

Tapping his fingers on the armrest of the door, he went back over the unfortunate incident with Amy. He honestly did not see her while attempting to make the bus. She was beautiful, but a highly emotional, quick-tempered female. Her tongue was sharp to strike and quick to bite. She was a combination of a snake and a wild mare, and he took glee in how much of a pleasure it would be to tame her. As the cab came to a stop, Aaron reached into his coat pocket and, leaning forward, dropped a twenty into the driver's hand.

Smiling, the cabbie tucked the money into his pocket. "Thank you, sir, and have a nice evening."

As Aaron climbed out, he nodded and shut the door. Entering his apartment building, the evening doorman was on duty, so Aaron wished him a good night.

Hearing the key in the lock, Paula knew her mother was home and walked toward the door, only to stop in her tracks.

"Mom, what happened to you?" Amy saw the concerned look on her daughter's face.

"I had a bit of a mishap, but I am okay. I need to go change, and then we can get dinner." Removing her coat and boots, Paula noticed just how soaked she was.

"Hey, Mom, I thought tonight we could make chicken and green salad." Amy at this point couldn't have cared less what she ate; however, she looked at Paula and smiled. "That sounds wonderful, sweetie. I will be back down in a minute." Heading up the stairs, she quickly showered and, slipping into sweatshirt and pants, embraced the warm feeling that went through her body. When she found her daughter, Paula was washing up the lettuce with the radio blaring and singing way off tune to the song that was playing, "Give me a sign, hit me baby one more time. Ooh baby, baby . . . ooooh." Chuckling, Amy walked over and turned the volume down. "That was . . . uh . . . very entertaining, although I think you play sports ten times better than you sing." Laughing, the two of them prepared dinner, with Amy listening to Paula's usual chitter chatter. "How was school today?"

"Oh, Mom, I have the best news. I made the after-school basketball team, and so did my friend Suzy. I guess her mom will be picking her up after the games, so that means I'll be able to get a ride home too. Isn't that cool?"

Amy nodded. "That is wonderful, and I am proud of you, honey. I always did like the fact that you got yourself involved in sports because you are very good."

"Maybe you will be able to come and watch some of my games."

"You know I will be there with bells on my toes if I can. But first things first. I need to find me a job, which is what I was out doing today."

"Any luck?"

Shaking her head, she sighed. "Nope, and it wasn't due to lack of trying either. It all comes down to experience and qualifications these days, which is why, young lady, finishing school is so important."

"I am going to finish. You know, school isn't all that bad. Are you going to be out looking tomorrow too?"

"I will be out every day until I find one, so welcome to my world. I have no choice in the matter. Things are different now."

Paula looked over at her mom with sadness in her eyes. "I know what you mean."

After dinner, Amy cleaned up while Paula sat at the table as usual working away on homework. Amy grabbed a cup of coffee, headed into the living room, curled up on the couch, and flicked on the television to catch the evening news. Tonight, though, she had trouble concentrating on the issues going on around the world as her mind kept drifting to Aaron. Lost in thought, she did not hear her daughter come into the room. Paula crawled onto the couch, cuddling up beside her. "Hey, can we watch a movie?"

"Sure, go put one in, and then it will be off to bed with you." The two of them cuddled on the couch, neither one of them saying a word. One was preoccupied with the movie and the other too mixed up and not in control of herself. When *Air Buddies* was finished, Paula leaned over, gave her mom a kiss, and bade her good night. "I love you."

Amy hugged her daughter back. "I love you too, baby, sweet dreams." Paula ran up the stairs, and Amy heard the bedroom door softly shut. Bed was not so far away for her either, and she leaned her head back and closed her eyes only for a moment.

The next day turned out to be warm and sunny. One would never have known that the day before had been such a wet, miserable one. Paula dressed in her favorite skirt for school, raced down the stairs, and noticed her mom fast asleep on the couch.

"Mom, wake up." Amy opened one eye and asked what time it was. "It is eight o'clock, and I have to leave for school in ten minutes." Pulling back the blanket and letting out a yawn, Amy got up and went into the kitchen to put on the coffee. She did not realize that when she closed her eyes last night, she would wake up on the couch. She must have been more exhausted than she had thought.

"Are you getting a ride to school?"

"No, I am catching the bus so I can sit with Suzy." Amy quickly made her a lunch, and just as she finished, Paula hugged her and headed out the door. Amy poured herself a cup of coffee and sat at the kitchen table, thinking about how to plan her day. One thing for certain was that she needed to hurry up and find a job as Nick, her husband, would not help out for that much longer. Finding yesterday's newspaper, she sat and went through all the help wanted ads, circling everything that was a possibility.

Sitting at his office, staring out the sixth-floor window, Aaron was still thinking about Amy. The buzzer went on his telephone, breaking into his thoughts. Leaning over, he pressed the button. "Yes, what is it, Nancy?"

"Aaron, you have a phone call on line 1. I believe it is your wife. Would you like to take it, or shall I tell her that you have stepped out?"

"No, it's all right. Put it through. Thanks." Letting out a sigh and running his hand through his hair, Aaron picked up the receiver. The last person he wanted to talk to right now was Beth. "Hello, Aaron here."

"Hi, it's Beth. I am calling to let you know that Adam fell off the monkey bars at school today and broke his arm."

Sitting bolt upright in his chair, he could feel his heart pounding. "Oh my gosh, Beth, is he okay?"

"Yes, he'll be fine. The school called, and I took him straight to the hospital. His arm was x-rayed and casted from wrist to elbow."

"Can I speak to him?"

"I'm sorry, he is lying down in bed. The nurse gave him something to ease the pain, but how about if he calls you back when he gets up."

"Okay, well, pass along a hug and kiss for me."

"I'll do that."

"Listen, Beth, thanks for letting me know. Is there anything either of you need, or something I can do?"

"No, thank you. We're fine, but I appreciate your asking all the same. Talk to you later. Bye."

"Bye." As he hung up the phone, he thought about his nine-year-old son. He hated being away from him, but he had come home one day to find Beth had packed up and left with Adam. After calling around to find out where she was, he had tracked her down at her parents, which was a five-hour drive. He made the trip out there hoping to bring the two of them back home, but she plainly told him she had enough of being married to someone who spent more time at the office than at home. She wanted to start a new life on her own with their son. Aaron was devastated but promised he would reduce the office workload. His family was worth it, but Beth was adamant that the damage was already done and could not be rectified. As much as he pleaded and promised, she was not to be swayed; and as he left, his son clung to him and cried. That was six months ago. Since then, he called Adam as often as he could and drove out to get him every second weekend and holidays. The phone call he just received deeply affected him. Picking up the receiver, he dialed his receptionist. "Nancy, I am going to leave the office early today, so could you please reschedule the rest of this afternoon's appointments for me?"

"Yes, of course. Is everything all right?"

"That *was* Beth on the phone, and apparently Adam broke his arm, so I think I'm just going to call it quits for the rest of the day."

"Ah, I am sorry to hear that. Hope the little guy is okay. Will you be back in tomorrow, usual time?"

"Yes, but in the meantime, I can be reached at home if anything comes up that is urgent. See you then." Hanging up, he grabbed his briefcase and coat and headed out the door. Normally he would hail a cab or take the bus home, but today he decided that enjoying the fresh air might do him some good. Walking home may not be such a bad idea.

Amy's first stop of the morning was at a diner not too far from where she lived. They were looking for a waitress; however, they wanted someone with at least a year's experience, which is something she did not have. Her second stop was at a florist, and although she knew nothing about flowers, she decided it was worth a try. They were looking for someone to help with running the shop. As she opened the door, a little bell rang, and a robust older woman came hurrying forward.

"Hello, can I help you?"

"Um yes, my name is Amy, and I am responding to your ad in the paper. I am looking for a job." The woman eyed her up and down, and then with a smile, she held out her hand and said, "Nice to meet you, Amy. My name is Deandra, but you may call me Dee for short." Turning around, she motioned for her to follow, and they went into a little room in the back. "Could I offer you something to drink? Coffee perhaps?"

"Yes, thank you, that would be nice."

Dee looked at her. "Let me guess, sugar and cream, right?" Amy smiled and nodded. While she waited, she looked around and noticed the shop was beautifully decorated with many floral arrangements and ceramic flowerpots. The walls were painted in shades of pink, and the floors were a natural, polished hardwood. It wasn't a highly prestigious shop, but it was tasteful and inspiring, providing a comfortable and cordial atmosphere. Setting the cups down, Dee sat across from Amy and asked, "So what do you think of the place?"

"I was just admiring it, and I love the way you have it set up. Very stylish, yet modest."

"Thank you. This is my dream. Ever since I was a little girl, flowers fascinated me. I would go out into the grassy fields, pick Mom pretty little bouquets, and bring them home. I am sure when I wasn't looking, she eliminated a few." Amy laughed, picturing it all.

"So how is your knowledge in regard to flowers?"

"To be honest, I know very little. I think they are very beautiful though, and some of them give off the nicest scents."

"Yes, they are like a perfume all of their own. What made you come in today to apply for the job?"

Setting her cup down, she looked at Dee. "I am a single mom and need to find work. Although I have no experience whatsoever in this kind of field, I was a cashier a long time ago at a supermarket, and I wouldn't think it is a very hard job to get to know. I catch on pretty fast." Dee looked at her and sensed she had been through a very rough time lately and decided to give her a break.

"All right, Amy. The job would be Monday to Friday, starting at nine o'clock in the morning and finishing up at five in the evening. The pay is twelve dollars an hour. The job is yours if you would like it."

Amy looked at Dee and nodded. "Yes, I would, and thank you so much."

"No need to thank me, dear. I am hiring you because I believe you fit the bill, so to speak. When can you start?"

Amy laughed. "Right now if you would like."

Dee chuckled and took her hand. "How does tomorrow morning sound?"

"Sounds perfect."

Just then the doorbell chimed. "You'll have to excuse me, but I have a customer. It was really nice to meet you, and I will see you tomorrow morning at nine o'clock sharp." The two of them walked toward the front of the store.

"Bye, Dee." With that, Amy opened the door and walked out into the sunshine.

With just landing herself a new job and the weather being so nice, Amy decided to do a little shopping. As the afternoon wore on, she looked at the time and realized she needed to get home as Paula would be waiting for her. Looking in shop windows, lost in thought, she did not see Aaron approaching. He startled her when he touched her arm, and she dropped a bag she was carrying. Bending down to retrieve it, he held out his hand. "Allow me." Picking it up, he held on to it. "Fancy seeing you again, and what a gorgeous day it is."

The expression on her face told him she was by no means glad to see him. "Do you always make it a habit to sneak up on people?"

Aaron laughed. "How about that coffee. Are you up to it?"

Shaking her head, Amy could not believe the nerve of this man. "How about . . . *not*. Actually, I was just on my way home, so if you would be kind enough to give me the bag back –" Aaron knew he had the ace up his sleeve.

"Ah, ah, ah. If you agree to have a cup of coffee with me, then I will return it, and you may be on your way."

Amy was furious. "How dare you. How dare you manipulate me like –" The rest of the sentence was cut off by Aaron's mouth covering hers. He could not resist as the little spitfire stood there with her hands on her hips, telling him off. Fully aware that she was being kissed, she pushed away from him. "You had no business doing that."

Aaron crossed his arms and grinned at her. "Well now. How about that coffee."

"After yesterday, I would have figured that you would have gotten the hint, but I guess you are not so smart after all." Amy stood there with a smug look on her face.

"Ah, the little she – cat wants to scrap, huh? Maybe I ought to put you over my knee and give you the spanking you deserve."

Amy took a step toward him. "Listen, if you so much as lay one hair on me –"

Putting his hands in his pockets with an amused look on his face, he replied, "Let me guess . . . you'll scream?"

"You know, Aaron, you are the most . . . the most . . . do you get a kick out of wasting my time? Just hand it over so I can be on my way."

Grinning, Aaron lit a cigarette. "As I said coffee first."

Letting out a much irritated sigh, she looked at him. "You know, I am really tired of playing your game. Fine, but just one. You hear me? *Just one*, and then I'm leaving with the hopes of never setting eyes on you *again*."

Winking at her, he bowed. "After you." And then they headed to the coffee shop just round the corner. Taking a table right by the window, it wasn't long before their waitress appeared.

"Are you hungry at all, Amy?"

"No, just the coffee please."

Leaning forward in his chair, Aaron stared at her. "So what did you do with yourself today?"

She did not want to tell him about her new job. "I went for a walk, did some shopping, and was enjoying the decent weather until it suddenly got ugly. How about you?"

"Ouch! As usual it was all work and no play at the office. And on the other side of things, there are no clouds hanging over my head." Aaron watched the facial play on Amy's face and was amused that he had managed to get her goat. The waitress returned, and Aaron sat there, tapping his cup as if deep in concentration. Amy focused on the lines in his face. "Are you okay?" He sighed and was not quite sure if he should tell her about his son. But what the heck. She made it quite obvious that she did not want to see him again. Taking a sip of his coffee, he said, "I got a phone call today while I was at the office, and my nine-year-old son had a fall at school. Needless to say, it resulted in a broken arm."

"Oh, I am so sorry. Is he okay?"

Looking at her, he noted the concern on her face and was deeply touched. "Yes, but suffering some discomfort from what I understand." Amy wondered why he was not with him at the moment. Not that it was her business.

"Have you seen him today at all?"

"No. No, I haven't. Look, Amy, I certainly don't want you to get the wrong impression of me, but –"

"If I may interrupt, Aaron, the impression I have of you already is that of a cad. No wrong impressions on my part, so please carry on." It took everything he had to keep his response to himself. "The fact is, my son lives five hours away with his mother."

"I see. You don't owe me an explanation. It must be very difficult for you. I couldn't imagine not having my daughter with me." Aaron looked at her questioningly.

"So you have a daughter?"

"Yes. Yes, I do."

"May I ask how old?"

"She's twelve going on sixteen, if you know what I mean." She said no more, and he wondered if she was married or single as her ring finger was bare.

"So what does your husband do?"

Amy hesitated. "He left about three months ago, so there are just the two of us." Both sat there silent.

"I am sorry. It must be tough for you."

The last thing she wanted was Aaron's sympathy. "Actually, it's not so bad." He could tell that things were not that easy, and she was trying hard to cover up the hurt. He admired her for that.

Amy looked at her watch. "Speaking of kids, I have to get going." Aaron left some money on the table, and they headed out the door. He gave Amy her bag back and fell into step beside her.

"Really, I am all right on my own. Thank you for the coffee, and I hope your son gets better."

"If you don't mind, I insist on walking with you." Amy shrugged her shoulders. "Okay, but it isn't necessary." They hadn't gone far before she stopped. "Well, this is my neighborhood, so thanks again." Just as she was about to walk up the path, Aaron took her hand and brought it to his lips. "No, thank you for a most delightful end to a quite boring afternoon." Amy was staring straight into his eyes again. Aaron let go of her hand, spun around, and retraced their steps. Standing there watching him, she noticed he was quite tall and nicely built. Giving her head a shake, she walked to the door and put the key in the lock.

CHAPTER 2

AARON WAS JUST pulling the house keys out of his pocket when the phone rang. Hurriedly opening the door, he grabbed the receiver just as the answering machine clicked on. Shutting it off and throwing his briefcase on the chair, he uttered a tired hello.

"Hi, Dad," Adam responded tiredly.

"Hey there, champ, how's my guy?"

"I broke my arm and had to go to the hospital. I have a cast on, and it is bugging me, but I can't take it off." Aaron could just picture it.

"I know. Your mom called me, and I wish that I could have been there for you. I've been thinking about you though. How are you doing?"

"Not too good."

"Aw. Hey, how would you like me to come and pick you up tomorrow so that you can spend the weekend with me?" There was a moment of silence.

"Okay. I miss you." Aaron's heart went to his throat as he missed Adam more than he could ever imagine.

"I miss you too, champ, very much. Let me speak to your mom for a minute."

"K. See you tomorrow, Dad. I love you."

"I love you more." In the background, he could hear Adam calling his mom to the phone.

It was a minute or two before Beth finally came on. "Hi. Adam said you wanted to talk to me?"

"Yes. I wanted to let you know that I am going to pick him up tomorrow around noon. Is that all right?"

"Sure it is. Are you just taking him for the day or overnight?"

"No, overnight."

"That is fine. Did you want me to put him back on the phone again?"

"No, not unless he wants to talk to me some more."

"Actually I don't know where he got to. He kind of scooted off."

"Don't worry about it, Beth. Just let him know I will see him around noon." After he hung up, he couldn't stop thinking about his son.

As usual, Paula was waiting for her mom at the door. Noticing the shopping bag, she took it from Amy and ran off toward the kitchen. Following behind and throwing her keys down on the counter, Amy watched as her daughter went through the bag to see if there was anything for her. "Mom, is this stuff all for you?"

Amy smiled. "Yes, honey, it is all my stuff. I have great news for you though."

Paula's head quickly came up, and she eyed her mother. "So what is it?"

"Well, for now on, while you are at school, I am going to be at work. I got a job today in a floral shop nearby."

"Mom, that's great, except you know absolutely nothing about flowers." Amy chuckled. "In fact," continued Paula, "I remember one time I brought you home a lily, and you said, 'Oh, what a pretty tulip.'"

Amy looked at her daughter to see her laughing hysterically. "Okay, Paula, that is quite enough, and I do remember that, but I have gotten a lot better."

"Are you sure you're not going to get fired on the first day?" Her daughter had the look of total innocence on her face.

"Very funny, Paula. I will have you know that I will be just fantastic at my job. Just you wait and see. Matter of fact, young lady, before long, I will be more knowledgeable about flowers than you." The subject soon dropped as the two of them prepared dinner. Just as they were about to sit down and eat, the telephone rang. Paula skipped over and answered it on the second ring.

"Hi, Dad," Amy heard her say and hoped that Nick would not ask to speak to her. A few minutes later, she hung up and sat down at the table. "That was Dad, and he wanted to know if I would like to go see a movie tomorrow night."

"So what did you tell him?"

"I said no because it was a school night, and I always have way too much homework. He said maybe we could go the following night then." Amy smiled at her. "Oh ya, and Dad said to say hi to you." Paula carried on eating her dinner with no worries while she sat there and played with her food. Nick acted like things were way too easy, but for her, the hurt went way too deep. The day Nick left, Amy felt like her world had come crashing down around her. She remembered that day very vividly, and since then, she had never been the same. She existed only for Paula.

When Paula went to bed, Amy stopped by her daughter's bedroom and said good night. She decided she should call it a night herself as tomorrow was her first day on the job. Slipping on her nightie, Amy opened up the night table drawer and took out a bottle of medication that had been prescribed by her doctor. Removing a capsule, she popped it into her mouth and closed her eyes for just a second. Picking up the glass of water, she took a sip, turned out the lamp, and crawled into bed. It wasn't long before the tears started to roll down her cheeks, and she cried softly into her pillow. She was not sure how long she had been lying there hoping she would fall into an exhausted sleep, but looking at the digital clock told her it had not quite been two hours. Rolling over, she knew it was going to be a long, restless night.

Amy awoke to the sound of the alarm continuously beeping. Reaching out, she turned it off and looked at the time. Seven o'clock. She knew Paula would be getting up soon as well. Swinging her legs over the edge of the bed, she reached for her robe and headed to the kitchen to get coffee started and lunch made for school.

Yawning, she felt like she could use another few hours of sleep. She had no energy whatsoever but hoped that working would give her the stamina she needed.

It wasn't long before Paula came down, poured herself a glass of milk, and grabbed a banana muffin. Joining Amy at the table while she was drinking her coffee, Paula noticed the circles under her mom's eyes and the tired look on her face.

"Didn't you sleep well last night?"

Amy looked at her. "Actually I did sleep okay, but guess I am a little nervous about starting my job today."

After she finished breakfast, Paula disappeared to finish getting ready for school. Soon she kissed her mother good-bye, wished her luck, and headed out the door. Amy slowly made her way upstairs, found a towel, and hopped into the shower. Closing her eyes and turning her face upward, she let the water beat down on her face. It felt so good, and she knew she could stay there forever. But forever she did not have. Climbing out, she quickly dressed and got ready for work. It was eight thirty-five by the time she stepped outside into the warm morning air.

Aaron had trouble sleeping the night before as he was excited at the thought of picking Adam up and spending the next three days with him. The drive out seemed way too long, and a few minutes before noon, he pulled into Beth's driveway. Just as he was getting out of the car, the front door opened, and he saw Adam running out to greet him. With a huge smile on his face, Aaron slammed the car door and held out his arms. Hugging Adam, he looked up and saw Beth standing on the porch steps holding an overnight bag.

"Hi, Beth, how are you?"

"Just great. Thank you for picking Adam up today. He was really excited about it all."

Aaron looked down at his son and smiled. "No problem. I am looking forward to spending the weekend together. I will have him back on Sunday around three, if that works for you."

"Not a problem." Handing him Adam's things, she watched them get into the car and waved as they drove off. She stood there for just a moment then headed into the house, closed the door, and leaned against it. She thought about Aaron and knew she still loved him, but not like she used to. They had met on a blind date when they were sixteen, and he had all the time in the world for her then. It wasn't until they had gotten married and he became successful at his job that things started to change. He spent way too much time at the office and very little time at home with her and Adam. That was the wedge that drove them apart, and she felt like she didn't know him that well anymore. It was not an easy decision to pack up Adam and leave, but she was not happy.

Amy arrived at the floral shop just ten minutes shy of nine o'clock and was met at the door by Dee. "Good morning, Amy. It is nice to see you."

Amy smiled at the kind woman. "And a good morning to you as well. I am eager to start work."

"Well then. Follow me." Showing Amy where she could hang up her coat, she offered her a coffee and showed her around the shop. "Now, you will be working the cash register, which you already are familiar with." She looked at Amy with raised eyebrows, expecting some sort of confirmation.

"Yes, I am."

"Now, the other thing that you will be doing is taking orders for flowers. Make sure you ask if the order is for pickup or delivery, write down the address, and it is all pretty much as easy as pie."

"I think I can handle that okay."

Dee patted Amy on the shoulder. "I don't have any doubt in my mind, dear, that you will do just fine. Tell you what though, when there are no customers in the shop, I will show you how to put some floral arrangements together if you like."

"Thank you. I would love that. Really."

The two women had no more time for chat as the doorbell chimed, and Amy's first customer of the day arrived.

The drive back home for Aaron went a lot quicker than it had seemed when he was going to get Adam. "What do you say that we stop at that little roadside restaurant and grab a burger or something?" Looking over at his son, he could see the beginning of a smile. "Okay, burgers and fries, Dad."

"Then burgers and fries it is." Adam talked nonstop about his broken arm and was thrilled when Aaron offered to sign his cast when they got home. It was almost six o'clock when they pulled into the apartment complex, and glancing at his son, Aaron guessed he was tired from the trip. Grabbing the things from the trunk, he took Adam's hand and walked into the building. As promised, Aaron signed the cast, and then they curled up on the couch together to watch *Star Wars*, which was Adam's favorite movie. "Dad?"

"Yes, Adam?"

"How come you never stay with me and Mom at home anymore?"

"Both your mom and I talked to you about it. Don't you remember?"

"Uh-huh, but all the other kids have a mom and a dad. I don't."

"Listen, buddy, you do have a mom and a dad, except I have my own house, and your mom has hers."

"Does that mean we are a famm-ily?"

"Yes, we sure are. You don't have to all live together in the same house to be a family. Take your grandma and grandpa Hillson for instance. They don't live with us, but they are still a part of your family. You go visit them at their place, and they come see you at your house. Does that make sense to you?"

"Yes."

"So are we clear on this now?"

Nodding, he slid down so that his head rested on Aaron's lap. Rubbing his sons head soothingly, it wasn't long before he heard him snoring softly. With a smile, Aaron turned off the movie, picked Adam up, and gently tucked him into bed. Putting his hand on the door handle, he looked at his sleeping son and knew that he meant everything to him, and he would not have it any other way.

Amy's first day at work was a busy one, and it was five o'clock when Dee finally locked the front door and put up the Closed sign. "You did really well today, and it was fairly busy." Amy was tired and wanted to get home to Paula and put her feet up.

She put on her coat. "Thank you, Dee. It was a terrific day, and I will see you tomorrow morning." With that, Dee unlocked the door for Amy, and she went on her way. Paula was eagerly waiting to hear all about Amy's first day on the job. She told her daughter how busy it was and how much she enjoyed her job. Paula looked at her with a smug look on her face. "So you do know what a lily is, right, Mom?"

Amy playfully threw a dish towel at her daughter. "Very funny."

After Paula was in bed, Amy went to her own bedroom and sat with her knees pulled up under her chin. She did like her job but was so tired by midafternoon that she was looking forward to home. Dee was a wonderful lady but way too talkative, and Amy just wished that she would be left alone in peace sometimes. Taking her nightly medication, she turned off the light, and it was a long time before she fell into a sound sleep.

Amy's second day at the shop was not quite as busy as the day before. Dee showed her how to put some flower arrangements together, and by the end of the day, Amy was able to make one on her own under the watchful eye of Dee. Being as it was Friday,

Amy had the next two days off, which she was looking forward to. At the end of the day, she bid Dee good-bye and told her to have a great weekend. She stepped out onto the sidewalk and proceeded to walk the fifteen minutes home.

The next morning, Aaron was already up and reading the paper when Adam sauntered into the kitchen rubbing his eyes. "Hey, good morning, sleepyhead."

"Morning, Dad." Aaron got up and poured a bowl of cereal with milk for Adam and watched him as he ate.

"So what would you like to do today?"

Slurping the milk off his spoon, he thought about it for a moment. "Can we go to the park and then for a big bowl of ice cream?"

Aaron chuckled and nodded. "Sounds good to me, so it's a deal. When you are finished breakfast, get ready, and then we'll head out."

They spent the better part of the morning at the park. Although the weather was slightly on the cooler side, the sun was shining. The ducks were wandering around, picking up the bread crumbs that the children were throwing out to them. Sitting on a bench, he lit a cigarette and blew a smoke ring into the air as he watched his son playing amongst the other children. "Mind if I join you?" Before he could answer, she positioned herself right next to him. "You wouldn't happen to have another cigarette?" Aaron looked over at his companion for the first time and wondered what her story was. Skinny she was, and her manner of dress was very gauche. The short colorful skirt barely covered her thighs, and the mesh stockings she wore left nothing to the imagination. Many necklaces adorned her neck, falling intimately into her almost exposed cleavage. He couldn't exactly define what shade her hair really was but knew he could pick out many. Hell, she looked like a walking rainbow. Reaching into his jacket, he pulled out a cigarette and handed it to her. "Thanks. Bad habit I know. Tried to quit a few times, but just don't have it in me. Keeps me sane and gets me through the day." Inhaling deeply, she continued. "Guess I'm gonna be a lifer, if you know what I mean." Shifting his legs, Aaron chuckled. "Yes, I do." He noticed the dark red lipstick stain on the tip of the cigarette. She had full lips, but the appearance of a pouter. Putting her hand on his leg, she eyed him up and down beneath a set of long thick, painted lashes. The smile she flashed was rather kittenish, and all he needed was for this cat to start purring and clawing at him. Feeling uneasy, he straightened up and gently removed her hand. "Look, whatever your name is –"

"It's Hilary, hun. You could just call me Hilary." He was interrupted from continuing when he saw Adam running toward him. "Had enough for the day?"

"Ya, Dad."

"Well, let's go get that ice cream then." Standing up, he turned to the young woman. "Enjoy your day." Taking another drag of her cigarette, she nodded. "You too, lovey, and thanks again."

"No problem." They went to the nearest ice cream parlor and then onto the toy store where they made many purchases. As they left, Aaron was just about to take Adam's hand when he saw Amy coming toward them. "Well, hello again." Looking at Aaron and then at the boy standing at his side, she moved her head slightly in acknowledgment. "Hi."

Seeing her glance, he said, "Allow me to introduce you to my son. Adam, this is Amy."

Kneeling down, she took his hand in hers. "It is very nice to meet you. I have heard a lot about you. How is the arm?"

He looked at her a little shyly. "It's all right."

Aaron glanced at Amy and asked her what she had been up to for the day. "Actually, I am just heading home from work."

"Oh, and where do you work?"

Amy hesitated, not sure if she wanted to reveal that piece of information. "Um, actually I work at the florist shop just down the street here."

He looked at her with a wicked grin and a look of amusement on his face. "Really."

"Yes, really, and if you will please excuse me, I must be going," she said. Saying good-bye, she walked off, leaving the both of them staring after her. With a hint of a smile on his face, Aaron put his arm around Adam's shoulder and continued on.

For the rest of the weekend, Aaron did not run into Amy at all, not that she was not on his mind. The truth was he could not stop thinking about her. On Sunday, he took Adam back home; and as he drove away, he was wishing that this was not the way it all had to be. He and Adam had an awesome weekend, but it ended way too soon.

Monday morning, Amy was back at work the usual time, and it was another slow day. Dee continued to chatter happily while she couldn't wait for her day to end. Putting her coat on, Amy glanced outside to see that the sun had disappeared. Saying good night to Dee, she opened the door, stepped outside, and ran right into Aaron, who was standing there with a smile on his face and one arm behind his back.

"What are you doing here?"

"Actually, I came to see you."

She glared at him. "You sure have –" And that was as far as she got before Aaron's mouth covered hers. She put her hand on his chest, and without thinking, she moved it up around his neck and kissed him back.

Pulling away from her, he stared at her with an amused look on his face. "Well, well. I guess you do have some feelings inside you after all."

Blushing, she wondered what on earth had come over her to stand there and kiss him like that. Just as she was about to say something, he presented her with a peach-colored rose.

"Have dinner with me this Friday night."

Amy looked at the rose and then at Aaron. "I don't think so."

"And why not?"

"Because I can't."

"You can't or you won't?"

"Both. Look, you are like a thorn in my side that I just want to get rid of."

"I wouldn't have ever guessed that the way you were just kissing me a moment ago."

"You kissed me first."

"Ah, but you kissed me back. So how about that dinner?"

She hesitated. "Thank you for the flower, it's lovely, but I don't think it's possible."

He looked at her and wondered if he had his work cut out for him. "Look, Amy, it's dinner. That's all. Do you think you can handle it?"

Sensing he was not going to give up, she finally agreed. "You don't stop, do you? Okay, fine. Dinner only, and that is it. Just so you know, I am only agreeing to this so that you will go away and leave me alone."

Aaron roared with laughter. "Dinner it is then." With that, he asked her for her house number and told her he would see her Friday night at seven o'clock. After he had left, Amy stood there biting her lip, not quite sure what to do with the rose. She had the urge to drop it on the ground, stomp all over it, and walk away but thought better of it and took it home.

The rest of the week went by quite fast for Amy. Some days were busier than others at the floral shop; and at the end of the day, she would walk home, hoping not to meet up with Aaron. She was still wishing she could get out of having dinner with him tonight, but she knew it would be over with quickly, and then hopefully she would never have to set eyes on him again.

She had just finished doing her hair when the doorbell sounded. Glancing at her watch, it was five minutes to seven. Giving herself one last look in the mirror, she headed nervously downstairs to answer the door. He stood there grinning, looking very handsome in his light blue shirt and black pants. Opening the door wider, she invited him in while she got her coat and was surprised when he presented her with half a dozen pink roses. Accepting them with a smile, she lifted them up to her nose and inhaled the fresh scent.

"These are beautiful. Do you mind waiting just a moment while I put them into a vase?"

"Not at all. We have some time."

Watching her walk toward what he assumed to be the kitchen, he thought she looked so elegant in her black dress and heels.

Helping Amy into her coat, they stepped out into the cool evening air and into the waiting taxi. They stopped in front of a very popular high-class restaurant, one that Amy knew she could never afford to eat at. Holding open the door for her, he ushered her inside and then let the maitre d' know that he had reservations.

"Right this way, sir." And they were shown to a very private table tucked away in the corner. Aaron held out the chair for Amy and then seated himself.

"Can I get the two of you anything to drink?" he offered. Aaron asked for a bottle of their best champagne, and she swallowed so hard that she almost choked.

"So, Amy, how was your week?"

"Work was very busy at times, but other than that, my week was great." The maitre d' promptly returned with two glasses and a bottle of champagne.

"Shall I pour it for you, sir?"

"No, thank you, just leave it on the table."

"Very good then, do enjoy, and a waiter will be with you shortly." With a slight bow, he disappeared.

Picking up the bottle, Aaron popped open the cork, which made her jump; and Aaron laughed. Handing her a glass, he watched as she slowly brought it to her lips while she eyed the other patrons in the restaurant. He was thinking how lovely she did look but seemed a bit nervous. "It's nice to get out and relax, isn't it?"

Setting her glass down on the table, she nodded. "It certainly is. I haven't been out for quite a while now."

Aaron handed her a menu. "Shall we take a look at it?"

Amy opened it up and was astounded at the price of the food. The look on her face did not go unnoticed by Aaron. "Have whatever you like."

Once their order had been taken, he reached across the table and took her hand. He couldn't help noticing that she was fidgeting and wanted nothing more than to make her feel at ease. "Enjoying yourself?"

Nodding, she picked up her glass and took another sip. Aaron, she found, was an extremely attractive man; and he dominated her mind. It was hard to make eye contact without feeling her stomach go into knots. She was brought out of her thoughts by the sound of his voice.

"Do you have an acquired taste for champagne, Amy?"

"Yes, I love it." He noticed she had a hint of a rosy cheek as she sat and twirled her glass. Reaching over, Aaron topped up her glass with more of the bubbly and then asked how her daughter was. "She is fine and spending the night at her dad's."

Dinner soon arrived, and Amy was feeling much more relaxed and talkative. They finished off the champagne, and the waiter arrived to take their plates and asked if they cared to look over the dessert menu. Aaron, raising his eyebrows, looked at Amy, who quickly declined. Letting out a little giggle, she put her hand on her stomach. "I think I ate too much, so I certainly do not have any room for dessert."

"No, thank you, that will be all for now."

"No problem, sir, just let me know if you require anything else." And he carried on his way.

"Our champagne bottle is empty. Shall I order another?"

She smiled. "I think not. If I have any more of it, I will not be able to walk out of here on my own."

Grinning at her, he leaned back in his chair. "You really are quite a petite thing, so picking you up and throwing you over my shoulders would not be a problem at all." Matter of fact, Aaron quite liked the image that he was conjuring up in his mind.

Paying the waiter, he escorted Amy out of the restaurant. They weren't outside entirely long before he let out a loud whistle to alert a passing taxi, and before she knew what was happening, he picked her up and threw her over his shoulders.

"Aaron, put me down this instant."

Holding her legs tight so she wouldn't kick, he opened up the cab door and dumped her inside. He slid in beside her and gave the cabbie the address to Amy's place. Looking over at Amy, he let out a devilish grin, only to have her laughing hysterically. "Did you enjoy yourself tonight?"

"Yes, thank you for a wonderful evening." As they sat there in silence, he wondered what she was thinking about.

He put his arm around her shoulders, and with his other, he picked up her hand and kissed it.

"Aaron, I –" And he touched her lips with his finger.

"Shush." Sucking in her breath, she found herself staring into those sparkling blue eyes. Wrapping his arm around her, he kissed her. Putting a hand up behind his head, she ran her fingers through his hair and totally lost herself in the kiss. Neither one of them realized that the taxi had stopped until the cabbie discreetly cleared his throat. Opening the door, they both got out, and he looked at Amy with a glazed look in his eyes. She knew what was on his mind and decided to ask him if he would like to come in for just a moment. Paying the fare, he put his arm around her waist and led her to the door. Taking her keys, he turned the lock and let her in. Flicking on a light switch, Amy removed her coat and offered Aaron a seat in the living room.

"I'm sorry, but I cannot offer you anything to drink as I do not have any liquor in the house." Aaron looked at her, not caring about a drink, but remembering the kiss that they had just shared. "I could offer you coffee or juice if you would like, though."

"I am fine, thank you." Slowly he got up, walked over to her, and kissed her again. Amy's insides stirred up feelings that she had not experienced in such a long time. She knew Aaron wanted to make love to her, and part of her wanted to also, but she did not know if she was really ready for that yet. Locked in each other's arms and lost in their own thoughts, they slowly made their way up the stairs and into Amy's bedroom. The moonlight was spilling through the windows; and very gently, they undressed each other, clothes carelessly falling into a heap on the floor. "Aaron, stop. Wait." Looking into her eyes, he saw a mixture of desire and fear. "What is it?"

"Aaron, I . . . I'm just not sure if I am ready for this. I want to dislike you, yet I am not sure if it is the effect of the champagne or . . . or –"

"Or?"

"Or if it is that I truly sexually desire you."

"Amy, love. Let your feelings out. You want me, and I can feel it in you."

"I don't know if this is the right thing to do. I have to be truthful to myself, and morally I don't know if I am." Rubbing her head, she hesitated. "Geez, I am so confused, Aaron."

"Kiss me, Amy, and if you pull away and it does not feel right, we will stop. I am not into the habit of forcing women." Tilting his head slightly, he found her lips, and the worries of that moment were soon forgotten. Pulling back the covers, he lifted Amy up and put her on the bed and crawled in beside her. Turning her onto her stomach and moving her hair aside, he kissed her neck, working his way down her back. The feelings she felt were beyond what she could express, and she knew her body was not rejecting his intimate seduction. Pulling her into his arms, he softly kissed her while gently touching one breast and then the other. Amy closed her eyes and, letting out a small moan, ran her fingers over his chest and down toward his stomach. Aaron's mouth kissed her breasts; and as he took a nipple in between his lips, softly suckling, it sent strong vibrations through her body. With a will of their own, her hands moved downward until she had grasped his manhood. She felt his body stiffen, and he let out a gasp. Sliding his hand in between her legs, she trembled with an urge so powerful as his fingers erotically teased her. A slight sob escaped her lips, and he knew he had the dynamics to tame her with his ravishing charisma. Lifting his eyes to look at her, he knew how hungry she was for passion. "Amy, tell me you want me, I know that you do. I just need you to say it." Although her words were barely audible, he understood. "I want you, Aaron, oh god, how I want you."

"That's it, love. Express yourself. How does it feel?"

"It feels . . . oh gosh . . . just don't stop."

"I have no such intentions. This is only the beginning of more to come. Pardon the pun." With that, Aaron eased her legs apart and, rising above her, moved in between them and entered his strong, aching manhood inside of her. Amy's head reeled from sheer pleasure, and as she clung to him, she heard her name whispered as if it came from a far-off distance. "Oh, Amy . . . so lovely and soft." Putting his hands on her hips, he guided her back and forth with such ease and skill. He took it slow, revelling in the sweetness, not wanting it to end as suddenly as it has begun. He could feel Amy's nails digging into his back, pulling him forward, wanting him. Seeking her lips, he tasted them with his tongue, kissing her face. Feeling utterly helpless, he plunged frantically, and it wasn't long before he heard her cry of release. Like a fast-moving waterfall, he spiraled and called out to her as he filled her body.

Lying on top of her, he could feel the sweat of their bodies and Amy's heavy breathing. Her hands moved gently up and down his back, making it feel like he wouldn't have things any other way. Gently disengaging himself and rolling onto his back, he pulled her toward him so that her head rested in the crook of his arm, and it was a while before she spoke, "Aaron, I'm not sure that this should have happened, and I don't want either of us to have any regrets." Raising himself up onto his elbows, he looked her in the eye and grinned. "Amy, we made love, and it was the most incredible thing we shared. I absolutely will not have any regrets and don't want you to either." With that he kissed her forehead; and together, cuddled in each other's arms, they fell asleep in the moonlight.

Aaron was the first to wake up, and he looked over at Amy who was huddled under the covers. Sliding over to her, he pulled the covers back and kissed her neck and softly rubbed her back. Opening her eyes, she looked at Aaron and asked what time it was.

"Morning, sleepyhead. It is twenty past ten." She let out a sigh and lay there without speaking or moving. Looking at her, he thought she looked like an angel in the morning light. "Amy, are you all right?"

"Yes, why?"

Leaning over, he brushed a strand of hair off her face. "We spent the night together, and I was wondering if you were feeling any better about it now."

Directing her eyes on him, she saw the tenderness and concern in his face. "I don't really know what came over me, but I am definitely okay. Thank you for your concern." At first she was hoping to never see him again, and the next thing she is in bed with him. All she knew was that she had butterflies in her stomach and felt content. She wanted to ask him how it had been for him but thought better of it as he looked like the cat that got the cream bowl. Just as she was about to get up, Aaron pulled her back down and nuzzled her ear.

Amy giggled. "Aaron, we can't possibly stay here all day." He did not respond; instead, he kissed her and then touched her cheek tenderly. He saw the response in her eyes, so he slowly moved his hand down her body, lightly touching her pelvic area. He felt Amy arch her back and gently move in rhythm as he massaged her. He could feel the heat coming from her body, and just when she thought she was going to burst from the feelings he stirred up inside her, he gently entered her.

Amy and Aaron went out for lunch, and they carried on like two high school students. He thought she looked absolutely radiant and wished he could spend the entire day with her, but she was expecting Paula home soon. After lunch, he walked her back home, kissed her good-bye, and asked her to give him a call sometime over the next day or so. Promising him that she would, she waved and watched him walk away.

Letting herself into the house, she decided to get some housework done before her daughter came home. After throwing in a load of laundry, she decided to tackle the dishwasher. Turning on the radio, she sang and danced around the kitchen while putting the dishes away. And that is exactly where Paula found her mother when she came home. Standing in the doorway, she watched her with an amused look on her face. Amy had not even heard Paula come in. Just as she was about to open up a cupboard, she noticed her daughter standing there with a questioning look on her face. Feeling slightly embarrassed, she turned off the radio and pulled the hair back off her face.

"Hi, honey. I did not hear you come in."

Paula chuckled. "I am not surprised since you had the music cranked right up."

Amy went over and hugged her. "Did you have fun with your dad?"

"It was awesome, Mom. Last night we went out for dinner and then to a movie. Then today we went for breakfast and then to the mall."

"I am glad that you had a good time."

"Dad bought me a cool new outfit for school and a pair of shoes to match." Pulling them out of the shopping bag, she showed them off.

"Wow, that is a really nice outfit, Paula. Nice shoes too. You will look sharp in that." Paula was just beaming. "Ya, and my friend Suzy is going to be so jealous too when she sees me wearing this."

Amy chuckled at the way kids were these days. Paula scooted out of the kitchen with her new clothes and headed upstairs to her room while Amy finished putting the dishes away. Looking at the time, it was four o'clock, so she decided to pop in a movie and lie on the couch. Her mind kept drifting to Aaron and the night before. Not being able to concentrate, she turned off the television and dropped the converter onto the coffee table. She paced back and forth deciding whether or not she should call him. Reaching into the pocket of her pants, she pulled out his phone number and stared at it. Biting her bottom lip, she walked over to the phone and picked up the receiver.

Aaron was at home sitting at his desk, trying to concentrate on some work he needed to get finished up for work on Monday. Tapping his pen, he couldn't stop thinking about Amy and the night they had just spent together. For a little spitfire, she sure was passionate, and he enjoyed making love to her. Matter of fact, he could not wait to see her again, and she seemed to have gotten under his skin. Throwing down his pen, he put his head in his hands and then got up to grab himself something to eat. He was just about to the kitchen when the phone rang. At first he decided to let the answering machine pick it up but then thought better of it in case it was Amy. Walking over, he picked up the receiver.

"Hello."

"Aaron?" asked the voice on the other end of the line.

"Yes," came the response.

"Hi, it's Amy. I hope you do not mind me calling you so soon."

Smiling, he could picture her on the other end fidgeting with the phone cord. "No, not at all. I am glad you called." He wasn't getting much accomplished anyhow. "Did Paula get home yet?"

"Yes, she did and had a great time. I put in a movie but could not concentrate so . . ." Aaron knew exactly what she was saying and chuckled. "I was trying to get some work done, but I am not any further ahead than when I first started." She didn't quite know what to say. "Would you like me to come over, Amy?"

"I really don't think that it's a good idea at the moment with Paula being home. I don't know how she will take it and all."

As much as Aaron wanted to see her, he understood. "That is okay, and I do understand. Maybe we could have coffee one day next week when you are finished work. How does that sound?" She accepted and then told him she had to go as Paula was coming down the stairs.

"Amy, I enjoyed seeing you very much, and I am glad that you did call me."

She had just said good-bye and hung up the phone when Paula came into the living room.

The rest of the weekend dragged by slowly, and come Monday, Amy was happy to be back at work so she could keep her mind occupied. It was now just into November, and there was a very chilly wind outside. People did not want to venture out for too long without huddling into a store to warm up. Eyes were stinging and watery; noses were numb and red. Amy had braved the weather this morning and walked to work but decided she would have to catch a taxi home. She was just finishing up with the last customer of the day when she heard the doorbell chime and looked up to see Aaron coming toward her.

"Hi, did you walk here?"

Shaking his head, he pointed outside to the waiting taxi.

"I was just about to call one myself. It is way too cold to walk home in this weather." Aaron agreed. "Actually, the taxis are busy, and the buses are jam-packed. You may have had quite a wait, you know." He grinned at her. "I am more than willing to share mine with you though."

"Well, thank you. That is very nice of you." He helped her into her coat, and as she pulled on her gloves, she said good-bye to Dee. The wind was still blowing when they stepped outside and into the waiting taxi.

"Would you like to go have a coffee or hot chocolate somewhere?"

Amy thought that she should really be getting home to Paula, but on the other hand . . . "Sure, that would be great."

Aaron asked the cabbie to stop at the little cafe over on the next block, and the two of them huddled inside, enjoying the warmth of the coffee. Neither one of them seemed in too much of a hurry to head back outside into the cold evening, but Amy needed to get home to Paula. It wasn't too long of wait for a taxi, and Aaron kissed her good night when it stopped in front of her house. He watched her walk up the sidewalk until she turned the key in the lock, pushing open the door. Turning around and waving to him, Aaron waved back as the taxi pulled away from the curb.

CHAPTER 3

FOR THE MOST part, November turned into a really cold month, and there was little sign that autumn had ever been. With the sharp winds, people were driving where they needed to go, reducing the normally high volume of pedestrians. The city buses were running quite steadily, which made the traffic grueling. Amy had been at her job for a month now and at times looked after the shop for an hour or two while Dee ran errands. Aaron stopped by once in a while after work, and they would go for coffee as they seemed to each have commitments that kept them apart some weekends. On this particular Tuesday near the end of the month, it had been an extremely busy day for Amy, and she was dead tired. To top it off, she had a headache and wanted nothing more than to go home and thought seriously about quitting work early. Leaning against the counter with her head in her hands, she winced at the sound of the telephone ringing and let Dee answer it. "Amy, it is for you. It's Aaron." Picking up the receiver, she was so glad to hear his voice.

"Hi, Amy. How's your day been?" Rubbing her temple, she sighed. "Well, I can't complain about it being dull, that is for sure. To top it off, I have an excruciating headache. Can't wait to get out of here actually."

"Ooh. That bad, huh?"

"Ya, that bad."

"Maybe you should just call it quits for today and take care of it."

"Thought about it, but hoping to ride it out. I'll leave if it becomes utterly unbearable. Anyways, what did I do to deserve this phone call?"

"Nothing actually. More like bad news. I have to go out of town for a couple of days for a business conference." She was quiet for a moment and then let out a little moan. "I know, Amy, I don't want to go, but I have to. I wish you could come with me. I was even hoping to stop by and see you after work, but I don't have time." Amy felt like her day couldn't have gotten any worse.

"When will you be back, Aaron?"

"Not until Thursday morning. I fly in tonight, have a conference to attend most of the day tomorrow, and then there is a dinner after that."

"Will you be able to call me at all?"

He smiled. "Are you going to miss me, sweetness?"

"Of course I am going to miss you."

He heard the break in her voice and realized that she wasn't in the mood for some gentle teasing. "Yes, I will call you as much as I can. I am going to miss you too, but I will be back before you know it." *Easy for you to say*, she thought. "Anyways, Amy, I have to get going but will talk to you soon, and I do hope you are feeling better tomorrow."

Saying a quick good-bye, she hung up and rested her head down on the counter. That evening when she got home, her head was still pounding; and heading upstairs, she ran a bubble bath. Clipping her hair up, she slid into the tub. The events of the day captured her mind, seizing her into a whirlwind. She had the feeling of being overtaken, and her breathing lacked its natural ease. She was suffocating. Tears rolled down her cheeks. She didn't ask them to. Laying her head back, she closed her eyes and thought about the last few months before Nick left. Things were getting a bit tense between them. He hardly came home anymore, and when he did, an argument ensued. Nick wanted her around to raise Paula and to be a housewife, which is exactly what she did for most of the fourteen years that they were married. Things never really bothered him until lately, and it seemed that no matter what she did, it was never good enough. Many nights she sobbed quietly into her pillow, thinking she had failed as both a wife and a mother, while Nick lay sound asleep beside her. He never saw the anger or the pain etched in her face, and she resented him for that. She hated that he slept so soundly, his body fully free of any remorse or blame. She had the urge to pummel him with her fists, to make him suffer inside the way she did. To make him feel trashy and worthless. She loved him, but he had become soulless of late. Letting out a sniffle and wiping her eyes, she lifted the drain plug and climbed out of the tub. How she had the strength to do so, she did not know. Slipping on her nightie, she took her medication and then went downstairs to say good night to Paula. Amy did not hear from Aaron until the following morning just as she was heading out the door to go to work. "Are you feeling any better?"

Covering up a yawn, she replied, "Just feeling a bit tired still, but at least the headache is gone." He thought she sounded a little under the weather and was a bit concerned.

"Listen, Amy, I have to run, but please take care of yourself. I miss you and will call later on tonight."

"All right, and I miss you too." After saying their good-byes, she walked out the front door, locking it behind her.

Aaron sat in a boardroom with fourteen other members, listening to the board of directors speak. He knew he should be focusing on the issue at hand, but he couldn't help thinking about Amy. He would rather be back home with her than here. He was brought out of his thoughts when he heard John ask, "What is your opinion so far, Aaron? We haven't heard your vote yet." Feeling slightly embarrassed, he tapped his fingers on the table.

"Well, I think the financial market will earn more money and grow, so I vote to buy other companies."

Looking around the room, many were in agreement, and he felt relieved. The dinner was held in a private dining room, and on the menu was prime rib. Finishing his wine, Aaron watched the men smoking cigars and talking about the day's meeting. He wanted nothing more than to escape to his room and call Amy. Thinking of something to say, he waited until there was a lull in the conversation. "Listen, gentlemen, it has been a bit of a long day, and I have an early flight out tomorrow morning. If you would please excuse me, I would like to retire to my room and get a good night's sleep."

Nodding, the men all bade him good night, and Aaron could not get to his room fast enough. Amy was helping Paula with a school project when the phone rang. Getting up, she walked over to answer it, hoping it would be Aaron. "Hello."

"Hi," said the voice on the other end.

Glancing at her daughter, she spoke softly, "How did the conference and dinner go?" She heard him sigh.

"Actually, it was as boring as hell. I finally had to make my excuses or I would have been stuck there all night."

Amy laughed. "Would that have been so bad?"

"Heck ya. Murderous actually."

"So what are you doing now?"

Leaning back on his bed, he loosened the tie around his neck and grinned. "I am lying here thinking about making love to you again and how fast I can get home to do it."

She let out a giggle. "You are terrible. What time do you get in tomorrow?"

"I should be back around nine in the morning, and then from there I am heading straight to the office. We could meet sometime after work if you'd like." She couldn't wait and was looking forward to seeing him again.

"That sounds wonderful." They chatted for a few minutes, and then she told him she had to go help Paula finish up her project.

"I've missed you, Amy."

"Ditto." And she hung up. Noting the look on her mother's face, Paula couldn't help but ask who was on the phone.

"It was just a friend. Let's get this project finished up and then off to bed with you."

Amy was awoken to rattling, and it took her only moments to realize it was the wind howling against the windows. It was the weekend and her day off, so plans did not consist of her crawling out of bed this early. Rolling over onto her stomach, she closed her eyes and threw the covers over her head, hoping to block out the sound. It was going to be impossible to fall back to sleep again. Sighing, she made a fist and punched her pillow in frustration. "Darn, all I want is to sleep a little longer." Moving onto her back with her arm across her forehead, she stared up toward the ceiling. Work was going well, but at times she just did not feel like she wanted to be there. For the last week or two, it had been so hard for her to get up in the morning and get herself ready. She was tempted to call Dee to let her know she wouldn't be in and then just go back to bed. Sleeping the day away would be easy to do, but leaving Dee to manage on her own when she needed her was not right. She owed the kindly woman more than that and felt guilty for the way she was feeling. It wasn't that she went to work every day because she loved her job that much; it was because she needed to work. The only money she got from Nick now was the monthly child support payment for Paula. Other than that, there was no other income, and she had to take care of her daughter's needs. She never dreamed that her life would end up like this, for if anyone had told her years ago that Nick and she would not last, she would have disagreed. He had been popular throughout school with being on most of the sports teams, and the girls chased him wherever he went. They had eventually become high school sweethearts, and he had been the only man that she had ever loved. Her parents liked Nick; however, her father insisted that they should wait before becoming man and wife. "Amy," he would say. "You are much too young to settle down right now. You need to finish finding yourself and live your life the way God intended. You are a bright, attractive woman and could go farther than what you are going to if you marry Nick right now. I can tell he is going to be the big shot of society, and you are going to be nobody. It is in his personality, his being."

"Dad, I am grateful for your concern, but I am happy. I don't want to keep having this conversation. Nick is the one I want for a lifetime."

Kissing her on the cheek, he stepped back and looked at her. "I have complete faith in you, Amy. I just wish you would wait, but the choice is yours of course."

Robert knew that sometime soon, he was going to have to give his daughter and only child to another man, and he wasn't sure he could do that. He protected her and loved her, but Nick loved her too, which was something he couldn't control. Amy was stubborn and very determined. Unlike a colt that could be tamed in a fashion to make him docile, Robert knew when it came to his daughter, it was fruitless. She was too high spirited. Nick was really going to have to hold on tight to the reins. The following August after graduation, they had gotten married, both at the tender age of nineteen. He took on a night job as a bartender in a fancy hotel lounge, and during the day he went to college with plans of becoming a lawyer. As for herself, while Nick had been in college, she took on a job as a cashier at a local grocery store until Paula had been born. Smiling, she remembered the day that she had found out she was pregnant. They had decided to wait at least a year after they were married to start a family. After being married for fifteen months, Amy got up one morning and was violently sick and extremely fatigued. Thinking it was the flu, she had spent the better part of three days at home in bed. Nick had been really concerned about her, so on the fourth day he made her promise that she would go see her doctor. Luckily, she was able to get in that afternoon, and it wasn't long after she was examined that Dr. Mackenzie was smiling. "Well, you are perfectly healthy, and I expect in about seven months from now I will be delivering your first baby. Congratulations." It took a moment for it all to sink in, and she could not wait to share the good news with Nick. After leaving the doctor's office, she went to a baby store and looked around. With a plan in mind, she purchased a tiny pair of yellow baby booties and left. Although it was really hard to keep the secret to herself for the entire day, it wasn't until Nick had come home from work and they were in bed that she let him know. First they made love, and then she snuggled up in the crook of his arm. "I managed to get in to see Dr. Mackenzie today."

"So did she figure out what was wrong with you?"

Smiling to herself, she played with his chest hairs. "Yes, nothing that is not normal for what I am suffering with."

"And what would that be?"

Moving away from him, she turned on the bedside lamp, opened the drawer to her night table, and presented him with the baby booties. Holding them, Nick looked at her questioningly for a moment, and then it finally dawned on him.

"I am going to be a dad?" Amy laughed and nodded. He let out a whoop of joy and kissed her. "Oh my gosh, I cannot believe it. I am going to be a dad. When?"

"Oh, in about seven months, the doctor figures."

And seven months it was. Amy was sick a lot until she was almost halfway through her pregnancy and ended up having to drop her work hours down to part time. Nick went to every doctor's appointment with her, and when the baby started to kick, he enjoyed laying his hand on her tummy and would talk to the baby. One night toward the middle of June, Amy woke up from a sound sleep startled with heavy pains. Realizing it was time, she woke Nick up, and they headed for the hospital. She endured a long, hard labor with him by her side, but after sixteen hours, they welcomed their beautiful baby girl into the world. Paula Elaine was so tiny and adorable and the apple of their eye. At Nick's urging, she quit her job altogether and never had to work again. Her days were busy looking after their daughter, and that was the way her life had been, up until Nick had left, and then everything changed. She was brought out of her thoughts by the ringing of the phone. Glancing at the time, it was only seven thirty. Answering it, she was surprised to hear her mother's voice on the other end.

"Hello," said Laina Gordon.

"Hi, Mom. What are you doing up so early in the morning?"

"Well, I have been up most of the night to tell you the truth. Your dad had a heart attack last night and is in the hospital."

Amy jumped out of bed. "Oh god, Mom. Is he okay? Why didn't you call me?"

"Listen, try not to panic. I didn't call you until I had some concrete information to give you. He is on the coronary care unit right now."

"How long is he going to be in the hospital?"

Laina hesitated. "I am not sure, honey. It will all depend on how your dad responds to treatment, and from what I understand, they may need to run more tests. Could be a few days yet before he is out."

"Oh, Mom, I wish you had have called me. I am going to go get dressed, wake Paula up, and then come out."

"Amy, your father is sleeping right now, so –"

"Mom, I will be there in less than three hours. Are you still at the hospital or at home?"

"No, I am at home right now. The doctor said I may as well as nothing I can do at this point. I do plan on going back up there though."

"Listen, stay where you are and have a nap or something. Paula and I will come by the house and pick you up."

Laina knew she could use some sleep, but she hated to leave her husband. "All right, I'll wait for you."

"Okay, Mom, see you in a bit. I love you."

"I love you too, dear."

Amy hung up the phone and felt like she had been hit with a ton of bricks. She couldn't believe her dad, whom she always thought of as being very healthy, had had a heart attack. Jumping into her clothes, she hurried down the hallway to wake up her daughter. It was almost ten fifteen when Amy pulled up in front of her mother's house. After knocking on the door several times, she finally took out her key and let herself and Paula in. Looking around, she did not see her mother, so they headed to the bedroom to find her sound asleep. Putting her index finger to her lips, she motioned for her daughter to not make a sound and softly shut the door. Putting on the kettle, she made herself a cup of tea while Paula sat on the couch with Tasha on her lap, her grandparents' old grey cat. Tasha had come to live at the house years ago when she was a kitten and had been spoiled ever since. Laina finally made her way into the kitchen as Amy was enjoying her second cup of tea and reading the newspaper. Seeing her daughter, she quickly held out her arms. "Oh, my dear, I did not hear you at all." Getting up, Amy walked over to her mother and hugged her.

"That is okay, you needed the sleep."

Hearing her grandmother, Paula left Tasha on the couch and walked into the kitchen.

"Hello, Grandma."

"Hi, sweetie."

Amy looked at her mother and asked if she was ready to go back up to the hospital.

"Why, yes, anytime you are. Just let me grab my coat and purse."

Although the hospital wasn't that far away, it seemed like it took forever to get there. They headed up to the third floor but had to wait outside Robert's room as a nurse was tending to him. It wasn't long before she came out and spoke with them. "You may go in and see him now."

Laina rushed over to her husband's side and saw his eyes flutter open. "Hello, Robert. Amy and Paula are here to see you." Amy moved closer and kissed him on the forehead. "Hi, Dad. How are you feeling?" She knew her voice sounded shaky, but as upset as she was, she could not stay calm.

"A little rough around the edges right now, but I don't plan on going anywhere just yet."

She smiled at him. "You are too ornery for that. Besides, we all need you around for a lot longer." With a weak chuckle, he patted her hand. Amy noticed he was looking very pale and tired. Robert looked over at his granddaughter.

"How's my little peach doing? Come and give your dear old grandpa a kiss."

Paula walked over to the bed and sat down alongside him. "I am fine, Grandpa. When are you going to be better?"

"Well, right now I am getting as good as care as any. How's school going for you anyways?"

"It's fine. I am on the after-school basketball team, and I signed up for noon-hour floor hockey."

He chuckled. "I guess we've got ourselves a little athlete in the family, eh?" And he winked at her. They didn't stay too long as they could see how much he needed his rest. Saying good-bye to her father, Amy told him to take care, and she would see him again soon. "I love you, Dad."

Turning his head, Robert looked at his daughter. "I love you too, peanut."

As she walked out into the hallway and left the hospital, she had no idea that once again, her world was about to change. When Amy arrived at her mother's house, she offered to stay for the rest of the weekend, but Laina would not hear of it.

"Listen, you and Paula just go on home. I will be fine, and I could really use some more rest."

Amy hugged her mother. "If you need anything at all, I want you to call me."

Laina stood and waved good-bye as they drove off. Closing the door, she picked Tasha up and went into her bedroom to lie down. With the cat curled up beside her, she shut her eyes but didn't care if she fell asleep or not. She just wanted to be alone, and time was all she had.

Amy and Paula drove back home in silence. While her daughter looked out the window, Amy thought about her dad. Robert Gordon had been a grade twelve high school science teacher and had met his future wife, Laina, when she became the new grade eleven English teacher. After dating for two years, they got married; and within the first year, they welcomed Amy Carys Gordon into the world. Laina's labor and delivery did not go all that smoothly, so no more children followed. Although her upbringing had been a strict one, Amy was extremely close to her dad and was the center of his world. Robert had always been an attractive man, rather tall and slim, and carried himself well. Her parents over the years had a loving relationship and, now that they had both retired, are never without each other's company. She couldn't imagine what her mom was going through now. Pulling into her driveway, she turned off the ignition and leaned her head against the steering wheel. Just as Amy walked into the house, the phone rang. Rushing to grab it, she heard Aaron's voice on the other end. "Hi, Amy. I have been trying to get you all day."

She dropped her purse onto the counter. "I have been out, and it has not been a good day."

"Okay, lay it on me. Is something wrong?"

Running her hand through her hair, she let out a deep breath. "Yes, matter of fact, there is. Paula and I went to see my father. He had a heart attack last night."

Aaron was silent for a moment. "Oh gosh, Amy, I am so sorry. Is he going to be okay?"

"So far, yes, but I am not sure when he will be coming home."

"Wow. Would you like me to come over, or is there anything that you need, Amy? Just tell me what I can do for you."

"Thank you, Aaron. You are so sweet, and I appreciate the offer, really. I have been pretty shaken up, but I feel a lot better now that I have seen him. Frankly, I was pretty upset with my mother though. The heart attack happened last night, and she only let me know this morning."

"Well, don't be too hard on her, Amy. I am sure her reasons are valid to her."

"That is my father, and how dare she keep something like that from me until now. I had just as much right to be there with him as she did."

"Look, settle down. You haven't a clue what happened those hours before she called you, and unless you walked in her shoes, don't judge too harshly. Maybe once your father is back home again, kindly ask her about it and accept her answer for what it is. For now though, forget about it as you're just upset."

"You're right. I am being petty and selfish. I do admit though that a hug would be great right about now."

"Are you sure you don't want me to come over and give you one? I can be there in an instant."

"Really, I will be fine, and what I need is to get my thoughts together. Maybe have a nice hot bath."

"Hey, I could come over and wash your back for you." She chuckled, and it almost seemed like a good idea. He broke into her thoughts. "Listen, Amy, if you change your mind at all or you need anything, I want you to promise to call me. Day or night."

"I will, and you never know, I may need to take you up on that offer. I had better go as it feels like I have put in a full day already. My energy is spent."

Aaron told her he would call tomorrow to check in with her. She went upstairs and knocked on Paula's bedroom door. Peeking in, she saw her lying on her bed, listening to her Walkman. Closing the door, she went to run a bath; and as her body made contact with the water, she let out a huge breath.

The ringing of the telephone woke Laina up. Glancing at the time, it was four thirty in the morning. Finally on the fifth ring, she leaned over and picked up the receiver. "Hello," she said in a quite sleepy voice.

"Is this Mrs. Gordon?" asked the soft-spoken voice on the other end of the phone.

"Yes, this is she."

"Mrs. Gordon, this is Nurse Ramsey from CCU. Your husband is not responding to treatment like we had hoped. Some tests had to be run, and he will need to go in for bypass surgery as soon as possible. There are some forms that need to be filled out. I am sorry to disturb you, but they need to be done right away. Are you able to come to the hospital?"

"Um, yes, I will be there shortly." After hanging up, she thought about calling Amy but then decided she just needed to get going. She was worried. Quickly changing into her clothes, she put on her coat, grabbed her keys, and headed out the door.

The nurse was waiting at the front desk when Laina appeared. "Mrs. Gordon, I will just need you to fill out the information and then sign on the bottom. Your husband is being prepared for surgery; however, you will be able to see him before he goes in." Picking up the pen, Laina nodded and then stared at the papers. She was wishing she had called Amy now. The forms took her about fifteen minutes to complete, and after handing them back to the nurse, she was told to have a seat. It wasn't long before the doctor approached and sat beside her. "Mrs. Gordon, I am Dr. Brighton, one of the cardio surgeons here at the hospital. I just want to go over a few things with you. The surgery your husband is undergoing is called coronary artery bypass, which takes about two to five hours, depending on how smoothly it goes. We are going to open his chest through a cut down the middle of the breastbone, extending into the upper part of the abdomen. At this time, another surgeon will be there removing a length of vein from the leg, which will be used to bypass the narrowed section of artery. Do you have any questions or concerns so far?"

"I don't know how this all could have happened."

Patting her hand, he took out a pen and a piece of paper. "My best work is that of a surgeon, not as an artist, but I will do my best here to illustrate for you how a heart attack can occur. Okay, picture this as the heart, and over time the inner walls of the coronary artery build up with a material called plague, which is this. Eventually, a section of this plague can break open, causing the formation of a blood clot; and if the clot becomes large enough to cut off most or all of the blood flow through the artery, a heart attack occurs. The heart needs a supply of blood, and when less blood is able to get through, it causes areas of the heart muscle to die. This surgery is performed after drug treatment fails to improve the blood flow."

"Are there any risks to this . . . this bypass surgery?"

"I am not going to lie to you, Mrs. Gordon. Like any surgery, there can be complications. Uh, such as infection, breathing problems, postoperative bleeding, heartbeat irregularities. We just need to keep our fingers crossed and hope for the best. Can you think of anything else you would like to know?"

"Not that I can think of. It is all too much for me to take in right now. What I'd really like is to see my husband."

"I understand completely. I will take you to see him. Follow me." Walking into his room, she stood by his bed and noticed he was hooked up to an intravenous drip and looked pale. Taking his hand, he opened his eyes and looked at her. "Ah, my Laina. I haven't been sleeping so well without you beside me." She missed him too. "Won't be long though before I will be back home with you."

Bending over, she kissed him on the cheek. "I can't wait for you to come home either. Tasha misses you. She walks around the house meowing." For the rest of the time together, they held hands with no conversation, each left to their own thoughts. It was twenty past five when the surgeon came in and told them it was now time to take him down to OR. Still holding hands, Laina walked beside him onto the elevator and down to the second floor. Just outside the surgery door, they were left alone.

"Laina, I love you. Always have and never regretted making you my wife."

With tears in her eyes, she looked at him. "Robert, you shouldn't be saying those things. You will come out of this just fine, and I love you too. I will be waiting right here for you when you come out. That I promise you."

The doctor reappeared with his clipboard and, putting it on the foot of the bed, lifted the breaks on the bed and wheeled Robert through the surgical doors. Robert never saw the panic in Laina's face nor the tears that streamed down her face as she watched him disappear.

Torn between whether or not to call Amy, she decided to curl up in the lounge and wait for news. The surgery seemed to take a long time, but just under five hours later, the surgeon came to see her. Removing the mask from his face, he rubbed his eyes and stared at her, knowing this was never the easy part of his job.

"I'm sorry, Mrs. Gordon, but the surgery just did not go well. We had your husband on a heart-lung machine for breathing and circulation during the surgery. However, he sustained heavy bleeding and breathing complications; and unfortunately, although we did everything we could, we were not able to save him. He passed away twenty minutes ago." Laina sat there speechless, and every part of her felt numb, except the storm that brewed in her eyes, and it wasn't long before they all came down her face in a torrential force of pain and grief.

"Is there anyone that you would like us to call for you?"

"Yes. Yes, there is. My daughter."

Amy had been trying to call her mother that morning for the last hour and a half. Unable to reach her, she figured she was sleeping in or had gone up to the hospital. When the phone rang at almost quarter to eleven, she was expecting to hear her mother's voice on the other end.

"Hello, is this Amy Munro?"

Puzzled, she said, "Yes, this is she."

"Amy, this is Nurse Ramsey, and I am here with your mother at the hospital. Your father had emergency bypass heart surgery earlier this morning, and unfortunately, he did not make it. He passed away on the operating table a little over half an hour ago."

Amy opened her mouth to say something, but no words would come out. All she did was stutter, "I-ah-ah . . ." And hanging up, she ran upstairs and hysterically banged on Paula's door. Falling down on her knees in the hallway, she rocked back and forth with tears streaming down her cheeks. That is how Paula found her.

"Mom? Mom . . . what is wrong?" Amy looked at her with wide eyes, still not able to speak. "What is it? Is it Grandpa?" Amy stopped rocking and nodded her head. "Did something happen to him?" She nodded her head. Quietly Paula asked, "Grandpa didn't die, did he?" When Amy put her head in her hands and sobbed, Paula knew. Just then the phone rang. Not wanting to leave her mother, she thought about not answering it. Running down to her mother's bedroom, she picked it up.

"Hello."

"Hello, is Amy there please?" asked a very male voice on the other end.

"Um, yes, she is but can't talk right now. Can I take a message?"

"Is this Paula?"

"Yes, who's this?"

"My name is Aaron, and I am a good friend of your mother's. Just let her know that I called."

"Okay. My grandpa just died, and she is real upset. I have to go."

"Hey, listen, I will be right over. Just stay with her." Although she heard him, she did not respond and hung up.

When Aaron arrived some fifteen minutes later, Paula let him in after he kept ringing the doorbell.

"Where is she?" Following her up the stairs, he found Amy just as Paula had, rocking back and forth on her knees and sobbing. Bending down, he gathered her in his arms and just held her. Brushing her hair back off her damp face, he kissed her cheek. "Amy, it's me. I am so sorry, baby. Everything will be all right. I am here and I won't leave you. I promise."

Laina left the hospital feeling like her feet were not even touching the ground. Unlocking the front door, she went to the phone and dialed Amy's number. It was answered on the third ring by Paula.

"Hi, dear, it's Grandma. Is your mom there?"

"Yes, hang on and I will get her. Some man is here too and says he is her friend, and, Grandma, I am sorry about Grandpa." Laying down the receiver, she walked down the hallway and told Aaron that her grandma was on the phone.

Moving himself away from Amy, he looked at Paula. "Stay here and I will take it."

"Hello, this is Aaron. I am a friend of Amy's. Is this her mother?"

"Yes, this is Laina Gordon. Where is my daughter?"

"She is here, but she is not very coherent at the moment. Is there a message that I can pass on to her?"

"Well, I-we-are going to have to make funeral arrangements, and I wanted to talk to her about it."

Aaron thought for a moment. "Listen, I can take the day off tomorrow and bring Amy to see you if you'd like. I will give her the message, but I don't know if she will be up to calling tonight."

"Tomorrow would be fine. Perhaps around noon."

"Noon it is then."

"Thank you, Aaron. Take care of my daughter, will you?"

"You have my absolute word on it, Mrs. Gordon." Hanging up the phone, he scooped Amy up in his arms, carried her to the bedroom, and gently laid her down. Covering her up with a blanket, he crawled in beside her and held her in his arms until she fell into an exhausted sleep.

Aaron softly got out of bed and went downstairs to find Paula sitting at the kitchen table. "Hi there. Do you have any coffee or tea?"

"Ya, both are in the cupboard next to the stove."

She made no move to get up. "Do you mind if I make myself a cup? Sure could use one." "Help yourself."

He put on the kettle, and after making himself some tea, he sat down next to her. "Your mom is sound asleep, and it is what she needs right now."

"So how long have you known her?"

"Uh, awhile now. I bumped into her one day by accident, and she landed in a puddle." He smiled at the memory, and Paula remembered the day she had come home soaked, and it made sense.

"So are you dating then?"

He knew it was not his place to discuss their relationship. "No, we are just friends. I am helping her get through a rough time right now, just like you will seek out your friends for support." Looking at her, he continued, "Everybody needs someone, you know, especially at a time like this. You doing okay?"

Paula nodded but said nothing.

"Let me know if you need anything, all right? Hey, why don't you and I go see what is on TV. What do you say?"

"Sure, but there is not usually much on, especially Sundays." She led the way into the living room, and the two of them sat there in silence, each absorbed in thought. Although the television was on, neither of them really paid attention.

It was a little over an hour later that Amy finally woke up. Realizing that Aaron was no longer beside her, she slid out of bed. Finding him in the living room with Paula concerned her as she wondered how at ease she was with him. Seeing Amy come into the room, he quickly got up and put his arms around her. "Can I get you a cup of something?"

"A cup of tea would be nice, but I can get it." Walking with her to the kitchen, he pulled out a chair.

"Amy, sit down, and I will make it for you. Just take it easy."

"Aaron, about Paula –" And he cut her off.

"Things are okay. She asked if we were dating, and I told her we were just friends. It's all good, so no need to worry."

Sitting down beside her, he took her hand. "How are you feeling?"

He could tell that she was bereft. "I don't know how I am feeling. Empty, I think. I cannot believe my dad is gone. It is something you wonder if you will ever get over. You know?"

He nodded. "I do know, and you will get over it in time."

"If you will excuse me, I want to go take a shower."

He kissed her on the cheek and told her he would be there when she came down. Making her way up the stairs, she stripped out of her clothes and stepped into the shower.

Aaron could hear the water running and was getting concerned. Amy was taking a long time in the shower, and he decided he should check on her. When there was no response to his knocking on the bathroom door, he tried the handle and was relieved to find it unlocked. Opening the shower door, he saw Amy huddled inside on her knees, crying and just letting the water fall over her. Reaching in, he turned off the shower, wrapped a towel around her, and helped her out. She fell against him sobbing uncontrollably, and he just held her. "Sweetheart, you're going to be okay."

"No, I'm not. I want my dad. I miss him. I . . . I . . . can't bear this."

Taking her into the bedroom, he sat beside her on the bed. "Listen, love. Grief is a natural response to the loss of someone that is close to you, and at times you are going to feel like you cannot cope. Try to think of it as the seasons, you know, spring, summer, autumn, and winter. They all change. Life changes, and just like the seasons change, so will you as you learn to cope. I didn't know your dad at all, but I would guess that he would want you to carry on, remembering all the good times. He may not be here for you to see him, but he will always be in your heart, and that is not so far away. You just have to reach out and touch it, and you will feel him."

"Oh, Aaron, you make it all sound so easy, but it's not. You didn't lose your dad, I did."

He rubbed her hair. "That is where you are wrong, Amy. I did lose my dad. Matter of fact, I lost my mother also. They died about six years ago in a car accident. They were hit by a drunk driver, and my father passed away at the scene, but my mother hung on for another three hours. It was the hardest thing that I ever had to go through."

With tears still running down her face, she snuggled closer against his chest. "I am so sorry, I didn't know."

"It is not your fault. You couldn't have known. But I realized what was making it all so hard. Every morning when I woke up, I was in denial, and that is how I spent my day. It was my way of coping, or at least that is how I thought I should cope, but it made me bitter and miserable. However, once I learned to accept what had happened, it got easier. Amy, no two people deal with grief in the same way, but I do know that in time, you will come to accept his death for what it is." Pulling her away from his chest, he brushed his fingers tenderly over her face, wiping away some of the tears, and softly kissed her on the lips. "Oh, Aaron, it is so hard losing a parent. I loved him so much, and I never thought of what it would be like to not have him around. Kind of one of those things you just don't want to think about, and now that he is gone, I feel so alone."

Rubbing her back, he was silent for a moment. "Being alone is a choice, and you can choose not to be, and I will be here for you as long as you need me."

She stared deep into his eyes. "I am so glad you are here."

"By the way, your mother called and wanted to talk to you about funeral arrangements. She is expecting us tomorrow around noon."

"Us?"

"Yes, us. I told her I would take the day off, and so will you be. I am going to take you and Paula over so that you can get things taken care of."

That night, Aaron stayed and slept on the couch; and Amy spent a restless night in bed, crying over her loss.

Just as Amy was having a hard time coping, so was Laina. Since getting home from the hospital, she sat on the couch with Tasha near her side and stared off into space. She and Robert had never been apart, until now, and she felt destroyed and abandoned. Even the house didn't feel the same. Never did she expect him to not survive the surgery. He was a good man, and it wasn't fair. As far as she was concerned, life wasn't fair, and she got cheated. Thank goodness she had Amy to help her as she would never be able to cope with the funeral arrangements on her own. Curling up, she pulled the quilt over herself and, with every descending tear, wondered how she was ever going to make it through her days without him.

The early afternoon air was uncomfortably cool with a touch of frost on the ground. The trees around were leafless and barren, and with the sun absent, the day seemed to match the mood of the mourners who had come to pay their respects. December had just begun, with Amy standing beside her mother at the graveyard, saying good-bye to the man that they had both loved and then lost. Neither one of them had made it through the day with dry eyes. Vaguely she recalled the days following her father's death, but her strongest memory was the sleepless nights and the tears that soiled her pillow. She was pretty sure that the well had run dry, until now. Beside them stood Paula, Nick, and Aaron. She had called Nick to let him know of her father's passing, and he was deeply saddened by the news for he and Robert had gotten along well. Robert Gordon was a man who was known throughout the community and well thought of. His manner of lifestyle was not elaborate by any means, so a simple service would be what he would have wanted, although the church was almost packed. Slowly the people departed to leave the family to have their own private moments. The casket lay on the ground, with flowers strewn all along the top. Aaron looked at the three women standing by his side. "Are you ready to go?"

Holding on to Paula's hand and wiping the tears from her eyes with a Kleenex, Amy nodded. She felt exhausted, and her head hurt. A lump formed in Laina's throat, but she did not answer. Trying her best to hold herself together, she walked straight ahead and, kneeling down in front of the casket, wrapped her arms around it and silently wept. Leaving her to grieve, the others waited; and it wasn't long before Laina picked up a rose from the top, brought it to her lips, and laid it back down. Gently standing up and straightening her coat, she took one last look; and then they all left together, never once glancing back.

Following the funeral, there was an open house back at Laina's house. The kind ladies from the church supplied the food and the drinks, and for that both, she and Amy were grateful. Skimming her eyes around the room, Amy saw her mother sitting on the couch with a cup of tea in her hands and a tight expression on her face. She knew her mother was feeling the loss and emotional distress, and understood. She just wasn't good with words. Walking toward her, she sat down on the couch. "How are you doing, Mom?" When Laina looked at her daughter, her eyes looked empty. "I didn't really know how hard it was going to be today. Saying good-bye and walking away was not an easy thing for me to do. I felt like I needed to stay with him so he wouldn't be alone."

Amy put her arm around Laina's shoulder. "Mom, you may think that he is alone, but he's not. Have you had anything to eat at all today?"

"Yes, dear, I had a sandwich." Leaning over, Amy kissed her mother on the cheek and got up. "Come and get me if you need me." Walking over near the window, Amy stood against the wall for support. She wanted to run and hide from the guests, but she knew her absence would be noted. The constant handshakes and words of condolence were starting to rip her apart. She knew this was a day she would never be able to blank out while for everyone else in the room, it would soon be forgotten.

When everyone left, Amy started to clean up when Aaron walked into the room. "C'mon. Do you have to do this now?" Glancing at him, his expression was unreadable. "Yes, I do. It needs to be done. I can't just leave it for Mom to deal with. Besides, it would do me good to keep busy."

"Ya, and you are going to work yourself into physical and mental exhaustion. It has been a busy day already, and you need to relax. We can clean this up tomorrow or get someone in to do it. I think you have had enough for one day. For a lifetime, for that matter." Amy clenched her fists and tried to choke back the tears, but they rolled down her face. "I don't need *you* or anyone else telling me what I should or should not be doing."

"Amy, listen. I –"

"No, Aaron, *you* listen to me. I just buried my father, and no one, including you, is going to stand here in this house and . . . and . . ."

Walking over to her, Aaron took her in his arms and held her as he looked straight ahead, his face ashen. He could feel her trembling as the tears of anguish wracked her body. For them, time stood still; and even as the quarter moon made its appearance amongst the stars, neither of them moved.

CHAPTER 4

THREE INCHES OF snow lay on the ground in St. Louis, Missouri, and another five inches were expected to fall. It was already late afternoon, and the wind was blowing the snow in all directions so that it made visibility hard. The tow trucks were busy with minor collisions and people sliding off the roads. Amy was not sure how it got to be December. Her mind of late was nothing but a mental block, like she had been in a coma, and trying to figure out the in-betweens was like trying to put a puzzle together without the pieces in your hand. But the feelings were still there. Dee had been extremely kind and allowed her to take the full week off following her father's death. Although she was back at work, she really did not know how she got through her days. She was so lost. Getting up in the morning was hard, and at the shop, she hated being around the customers for they were all euphoric and in the Christmas spirit. They shared their holiday plans with her, and she did not even want to think about it. Matter of fact, she had not even thought that far.

Aaron had been a pillar of strength, setting aside his personal and professional commitments to take care of her own needs. Amy felt so guilty, but Aaron would hear none of it. All he ever said was "Nothing is as important as your well-being. I don't mind in the least." She owed him so much.

Thinking about him, she picked up the phone and called his office. The secretary put her call through immediately. "Hi, Amy. Everything okay?"

"Yes, I was just thinking about the weather, and I am surprised to find you are still at the office."

Swiveling around in his chair, he looked out the window. "It is nasty out, isn't it? Are you at home or at work?"

"Actually, I am home and have been for a while now. Dee decided that it was best to close up shop. The weather was just getting worse. Are you heading home soon?" Putting his pen down, he was silent for a moment.

"I guess I should get going as I may not make it. I had some important work to finish up for a meeting tomorrow, which is why I am still here. If this weather keeps up, I will not be able to go pick Adam up this weekend. I had planned on leaving early tomorrow afternoon."

"I know it will be disappointing for both of you, but if your plans change, maybe you could come by the house."

"Amy, you can count on it. I'd be there right now if I could. Speaking of which, I had better think about getting myself home. I will call you tomorrow and let you know what is happening."

"I actually have an appointment tomorrow morning with the school. Paula's parent-teacher interviews."

"Is everything all right at school with her?"

"Oh, yes, of course. She is doing very well as far as I know, but they always have interviews before Christmas vacation. I am certain though that I may have to cancel as there is no way I will be out in this. Anyways, I won't hold you up any longer. Please be careful, Aaron."

"I will, sweetheart. No need to worry." But as she hung up, she couldn't help but feel uneasy.

Although it had stopped snowing, the next day was no better. Everyone woke up to almost eight inches of snow; the schools were closed, and Dee called Amy to tell her not to bother coming in. The road conditions were treacherous, and people were asked not to be on them unless they had to. Just before noon, she heard from Aaron, and he let her know that his plans with Adam were cancelled. He was going into the office for the afternoon and then would try to get over to see her. Needing to keep busy, she called her mother to see how she was faring. Laina was having a hard time being on her own now and didn't quite know what to do with her life. She thought about selling the house and moving into an apartment but was not yet ready to leave a home that held so many memories. Telling her mother to take care, she hung up. It was almost six o'clock that evening when Aaron showed up. Taking his coat and gloves from him, Amy offered him something hot to drink.

"A cup of coffee would be great if you have any made."

"Coming right up." And he followed her into the kitchen. "So, Aaron. How was your day?"

"It was awful actually. The meeting I was supposed to have didn't happen. The client said he would be there, even under the current weather conditions; and then about an hour before the meeting, he cancels because the weather was so bad. Go figure. I would have rather stayed at home today." Glancing around, he didn't see her daughter. "Is Paula home?"

Amy nodded. "Yep. She's up in her room doing homework. She will come out though when she wants something to eat." Taking their coffee into the living room, Aaron sat on the couch while Amy flicked on the stereo. Curling up against him, she took in his scent. Whatever he was wearing was not familiar to her. How she missed it when they were apart. She only half listened to the soft music playing as her mind was totally focused on the man beside her. He was six one to her five-six frame. He had the type of hair that a woman would love to run her fingers through-short, dark, and with the odd little curl. For his age of thirty-four, his physique was flawless and evenly toned. His complexion was soft, lacking in facial hair. She was definitely conscious of her sexuality, and he excited her. "Hey, I didn't get my kiss." Startled, she turned to look at him. He bent down and pressed his lips against hers with an urgent desire. Letting out a little groan, he moved away from her slightly. "I had better stop before I end up carrying you to the bedroom and making love to you."

Giggling, she stretched out; and this time when he kissed her, she ran her fingers through his hair then, slipping them inside his shirt, ran them down along his chest. Although it was hard to pull himself away from Amy without scooping her up in his arms, he had no choice. She was still not comfortable having Aaron share her bedroom while Paula was at home. While things were fairly under control physically for the moment, he decided that now was a good time to leave. Taking the cups to the kitchen, he put them into the sink and buttoned up in his coat. Drawing her into his arms, he held her for a few moments. "You have no idea what you are putting me through right now, do you?"

"I do know, and it's not fair, but it is probably best for the both of us if we said good night."

"Okay, I get the hint. You want me outta here."

"Aaron, I never said that. How could you think I – I take deep offense to that." His twinkling eyes and sheepish grin told her he was playing very amusing games. "I will call you tomorrow. Hope you sleep just as well as I am going to." With that, he gave her one last kiss and headed for the front door. As he was walking up the sidewalk to his car, she noticed that it had gotten colder out, and tiny icicles were forming along the edge of the roof and on the branches of the bare trees. With the night clear and the moon out, it made them look like crystals of glass. With the frustrated state

Aaron left her in, she had a strong impulse to smash every single one of them. Instead, she slammed the door shut and pounded her fists against it.

It was midafternoon the next day when Aaron received a phone call from Beth. "Hi, Aaron. How have you been?"

"I have been great, although I am not liking this weather we are getting right now. How about you?"

"Things are fine on my end, and our weather is not any better. Adam was disappointed that he couldn't see you, but he understood why."

"Ah, figured as much. I felt bad about cancelling with him, but the roads' conditions were awful, and I didn't want to run the risk. I'll come get him when they clear up enough. How is he anyways?"

"Oh, fine. As you know, his cast is off, and he is back to normal routine again. It was hard on him to be limited in some things when he is very active and all over the place."

Chuckling, Aaron tapped his pen. "I can imagine that. I swear that son of ours plays in his sleep. I'd like to know where he gets all his energy from."

"Well, I'm certainly not going to complain about it. Active is good. Anyhow, change of subject here. I was wanting to speak with you when you came out to get Adam. However, because those plans changed, I decided to call you instead."

"What's up?" She let out her breath. "I wanted to talk to you about us. I guess there is really no good time to tell you this, but I am going to file for a divorce." Aaron was silent. "I have an appointment with a lawyer next week."

"Damn it, Beth. Why?"

"Aaron, I left because I was not happy anymore, and I just don't love you the same way that I used to." Rubbing his forehead, a thought entered his mind. "Is there someone else in your life now?"

"It is not about whether there is someone else in my life. It is about you and me. We will never reconcile, and I just don't see why we should drag things out."

"What about Adam?"

"He will be okay. You're still going to always be a part of his life. You are his dad, and you can see him whenever you want to. That is never going to change."

"What changed, Beth, was when you packed up and left. We used to be a family, and I got to see him every day, and now I have to drive five bloody hours every second weekend to get my son. And that is weather permitting."

"That is where you are wrong, Aaron. We were *never* a family. Your family was at work. *That* is why I left. Listen, I know you are upset –" Her sentence was cut off by his words.

"You damn well better believe that I am upset." Throwing his pen across the room, he glanced out the window. "Look, if a divorce is what you want, then I will sign, but I plan on being just as much a part of Adam's life as I always have been. Don't take that away from me." Aaron heard the sigh of relief on the other end.

"I won't. I promise you that you will still have full access to your son. I don't want you to think that this is easy for me, because it's not. But this is what I want."

"Did you ever think to ask me what *I* wanted?"

She wasn't going to allow him to intimidate her. "I am not about to ask what you want, because *I* was the one that left you. I don't want this marriage anymore. I need structure in my life, not only for myself but for Adam. I am allowing my biological clock to tick right past me. I need a life expansion. Far more than what I have now. I don't want to have a face-to-face with you, Aaron, but I will if you are planning on fighting me on this."

"Fine, Beth. Do what you want. Just have your lawyer send me the papers to look over, and we will go from there."

"That's it? That's all you have to say?"

"What am I supposed to say, Beth? You call me up and dump this divorce stuff on me. You prepared yourself, but this was totally unexpected for me. I am not about to fight over this, so like I said, do what you want."

"All right then. As soon as I have anything for you, I'll let you know. For the moment, I guess we don't have much else to say, huh?"

Aaron was so shaken and upset that he just wanted to get out of the office. "I guess not, and, Beth?"

"Yes?"

"I do hope you enjoy the rest of your day, because you ruined what I had left of mine."

Dropping the receiver into the cradle, he put on his coat, grabbed his gloves, and walked out the door. Amy was in the middle of putting dinner together when Aaron showed up. The look on his face told her that something was definitely bothering him. Sitting down, she waited for him to speak.

"Beth called me. She is filing for a divorce." She watched him as he twirled his fingers.

"Oh. I see. Um, how do you feel about that?"

"I don't know, Amy. Shocked, I guess. I admit, she took me off guard, but it is what she wants. I always did love her and Adam, but I wasn't the one that left. I suppose I can't really blame her for that as I certainly would not have gotten a trophy for family man of the year." She reached out and took his hand. "I am sorry. This must be rough on you. What did you tell her?"

"I told Beth that I would sign the papers if that is what she wants. I guess a part of me was hoping she would eventually come back, even though I knew that would never happen. She figures there is no sense in dragging the marriage out, and she is right about that. It is not easy though to let go of the past."

Getting up from her chair, she walked to the counter and gripped the edges, her back turned to him. "Aaron, I never knew that you had any hopes of reconciling with Beth. I mean . . . if I did, I would never have gotten involved with you in the first place."

"Amy, listen. Don't take it that way."

Swinging around, she looked like a coiled snake ready to bite. "How am I supposed to take it then? Maybe we were wrong to get to where we are now. Do you think I would have done this if I had known what your feelings were in regard to your marriage? Do I look like I have *sucker* written on my forehead?" Her cheeks were becoming colored from her temper.

"Amy, I don't know why I said that . . . about hoping Beth would come back. I was just upset and confused, I guess."

"Well, you are going to have to deal with those feelings then, aren't you? I am not going to be caught in your circle. I am not going to be monkey in the middle. Now, if you will excuse me."

Aaron slowly got up and stepped toward her. "Amy, I do have feelings for you. I love you, so don't doubt that."

Covering her ears, she looked him in the eyes. "I can't hear you. La la la la la . . ."

"Stop that, for gosh sakes. You're acting like a child. I am only going to say this once. I apologize. I was upset, and how I feel is my issue. I am going through with the divorce, and I want to be with you. I'm not going to let this change anything. Let's forget this conversation ever took place and move on with our lives together." For a time, there was nothing but silence between them.

"I know how I felt when Nick left, but I would never go as far as wanting him back in my life, especially since you are now in it. However, I will overlook that comment, but it doesn't mean that I am still not angry with you for saying it."

"Do you love me?"

"Ask me tomorrow and you will get your answer."

"Amy, you stubborn brat."

Her face softened. "All right, yes, I love you."

Peering at the dish on top of the stove made him realize how famished he was. "Hey, something looks good. What are you making for dinner?"

"Ham casserole. I make a mean one too. Are you fishing for an invite?"

With a look of mischief on his face, he pretended to think about it for a moment. "Well, that depends what is on the dessert menu."

Amy ran her tongue over her lips seductively. "Considering that Paula is going to be spending the night at her friend Suzy's house, maybe you and I could whip up a chocolate cake." As she started to walk away, Aaron grabbed her and, putting his finger under her chin, lifted her head so that their eyes met.

"Not so fast, young lady. So are you telling me that Paula will not be here tonight, and you would rather play Betty Crocker in the kitchen?"

Looking at him with complete innocence, she nodded. "Uh-huh."

His mouth moved closer to hers. "Well now, do you have any better ideas?"

"Uh-huh."

"Like?"

"Well, I was thinking after we make the cake, we could clean up the mess."

"Oh, so you want to play little Susie Homemaker as well. Any other ideas?"

"Hmmm, let me see." Touching her finger to her forehead, she stood there as if deep in thought. "Nope, nothing else. I am plum out of ideas."

"Is that right now. Well, perhaps I can help you out then." And he lowered his head and kissed her.

Paula chatted throughout dinner about her evening plans at Suzy's house, but although Aaron and Amy were paying attention, they found it hard to concentrate. After dinner, while they were cleaning up, Suzy's father arrived; so kissing her mom and saying good-bye to Aaron, she ran out the door, eager to be with her friend.

Amy grinned at him. "So would you like to watch a movie or something?"

"Actually, I have a better idea. Since Christmas is just around the corner, why don't you and I go to the shopping center. We could check out all the decorations and what not. What do you say?"

"Ooh, that sounds like a great idea. Maybe Santa will be there, and if you are a good boy, maybe he will let you sit on his knee."

Aaron roared with laughter. "Any more smart remarks from you and we may just have to put you over his knee instead."

Although Amy hadn't been all that much into the festive spirit lately, she was glad to get out. She was amazed to see how many people already had their Christmas lights up and trees decorated. The mall shopwindows were creatively done with animated scenes and bustling with activity. An all-girls school choir was singing carols, drawing a huge crowd in the center of the mall. And of course, Santa was seated in his big plush chair, keeping busy with the lineup of children waiting impatiently to sit on his knee and help themselves to the candy basket. Aaron and Amy stayed until almost closing time and then went back to her place. Aaron turned on the gas fireplace while Amy made hot cocoa with marshmallows. Joining him, she handed him a cup.

"That was a great idea you had to go to the mall. I enjoyed myself."

"So did I. Maybe we should think about getting some lights up around your house sometime soon. What do you think?"

Sipping her cocoa, she hesitated. "To tell you the truth, I hadn't really thought much about it this year, but I suppose I should, for Paula's sake at least."

Pulling Amy toward him, he softly ran his finger down her cheek. "Come on, scrooge, you should get into the holiday spirit, you know, not only for Paula but for yourself too." Removing the cup out of her hand, he put it on the table and turned her face to meet his.

Amy looked at him and smiled. "Did I ever tell you that you have the most amazing blue eyes?"

Aaron let out a laugh. "No, not until now. Did I tell you that I think you are a beautiful woman?"

"No, not until now, and I didn't know there was such a thing as a beautiful scrooge. From my experience, they scowl and frown and are actually quite ugly."

"There is always an exception to the rule, you know. You are the only beautiful scrooge that I have ever known of." There was no light in the room except from the flames in the fireplace making shadows on the wall. They danced and flicked like they were entwining themselves together. Like they were rhythmed to do so. Aaron kissed her and then pulled away.

"I want to make love to you, Amy. It's been too long."

"I want to make love to you too."

Taking her hand, he led her upstairs to the bedroom. Gathering her in his arms, he traced kisses along her neck while he gently undid her blouse. "I want you naked . . . here . . . in front of me, Amy." She opened the zipper on his pants and lowered them past his hips until they fell to the floor. Removing the rest of their clothing, they kissed each other hungrily, bodies pressed tightly together. They explored each other's bodies with all the built-up desire of two people longing for each other. Taking her hand, he led her toward the bed. Lying beside her, he raised her arms above her head and allowed his lips to slide over her shoulders, moving downward, expertly exploring every nook and curve of her body. He wanted to know it all. Amy shivered in anticipation, and she felt weightless. Opening her legs, he gently teased and tasted her with his tongue. She was sweet and warm. "Jesus, Amy . . . you feel and taste so darn good." Amy's chest rose and then fell, and she could feel her heart race. In a husky voice, she said, "Kiss me." Aaron kissed his way up to her breasts and then to her lips, pushing his tongue into her mouth. She ran her hands down his back, and he looked at her with fueled-up passion. "Touch me, Amy." Feeling her way down, she came to the soft mound of curls then moved her hands up and down his manhood, feeling the droplets of moisture from his arousal. Groaning, he turned onto his side, gliding his hand over her belly, reaching the moist folds that he had just tasted, and slowly rubbed her flesh. Making contact with her most tender spot, she raised her hips and moaned his name. She quivered like a leaf partially frozen to the earth, with even the wind unable to release it.

He looked at her and saw that her eyes were closed, and she was biting down on her bottom lip. Knowing he was pleasuring her, he continued to rub while her hips moved in unison. It wasn't long before she shuddered and called for him. "Oh my god . . . oh my god . . . Aaron." Inserting his fingers inside her, he could feel the wetness and knew she had found release. Smiling, he rose over her and slid inside her. He heard her sigh. He tried to go slow and easy, but his body was wanting release. She felt so good. "Wrap your legs around my hips." His voice was husky. Once she did, that was the end for him. Rising up on his hands, he closed his eyes; and he took her, thrusting forward, burying himself deeper and deeper. "Come on, baby . . . Go with me here . . ." With one final groan, he spilled his seed explosively inside her as she fell in with him, coming once again. They lay there basking in the warmth and sweat of each other's bodies, so it was a long time before either of them moved. Rolling off Amy, Aaron lay down beside her and drew her close to him. Although this time there was no moonlight glowing on them, they were both content and, with that, fell asleep in each other's arms.

The morning brought her a sense of completeness, and she had no worries. Glancing over at Aaron, Amy assumed he was sleeping soundly. Gently pulling back the covers, she slid out of bed.

"Where are you going?" she heard a still-sleepy voice. Turning around, she was surprised to see he was awake.

Slipping on her robe and slippers, she eyed him. "I thought I would go down and put on a pot of coffee. You up for a cup?" With a lazy grin on his face, he looked her up and down.

"I would rather have some more of you. Coffee can wait."

Giggling, she walked out of the bedroom and said over her shoulder, "Meet you downstairs." And it wasn't long before he did. He thought about staying in bed; however, the smell of bacon cooking made his stomach rumble. Finding her standing in front of the stove, he came up behind her and wrapped his arms around her waist. Temptation had him nuzzling her neck and breathing in the scent of her hair.

"Are there eggs to go with that bacon?"

"Of course. And how would you like them?"

"Cracked into the pan and cooked would be nice."

Amy laughed. "Cracked and cooked it is then. Would you like toast with that as well?"

"Yes, two pieces would be perfect." Walking over to the coffeepot, he helped himself and sat down. Watching her, he liked the way her body moved around the kitchen, and he wondered just what she was wearing underneath that robe. He could feel his body stirring.

Amy brought him his breakfast, and while he ate, she sipped on her coffee. "How come you are not eating?"

"Ever since I was a little girl, I never was much of a breakfast person, much less a fan of bacon and eggs. Paula, on the other hand, inherited her father's appetite."

After the breakfast dishes were cleaned up, they both showered, got dressed, and spent the day enjoying each other's company before Paula arrived back home.

It was only three days before Christmas, and the stores seemed to be busier every day with people hurrying to get their last-minute shopping done. For Amy, it was no different. With the snow that fell the beginning of the month, it stayed; and with the ice on the roads and the coldness of the air, she did not care to venture outside any more than she had to. Even going to and from work, she took a taxi. Although the snow had just recently disappeared, freezing-cold winds still swept across the roads, making outside travel still unbearable. The sidewalks and roadways were littered with tree branches that broke, and you could hear the crunch as one stepped through it all. Finished work for the day, she decided she needed to get her gifts bought and some baking done. Laina was joining her for the holiday season, although she would rather stay at home, but Amy would have none of that. Aaron and Adam were going to be joining them for Christmas dinner as well, seeing as they had no other plans.

Aaron brushed the hair back off his forehead as he headed down the crowded highway. At this time of year, the traffic was heavy and moving at a much slower pace. Beside him sat Adam who was filling his dad in on the school Christmas play that he was recently in. "It was so cool, Dad. I got to be an elf, and I had to bring a hammer to school and a piece of wood cuz I had to pretend I was making a toy."

He laughed at his son. "And what was it you were making?"

"Well, I was making a truck, but it wasn't real. But I was one of Santa's helpers. That is what elves do, you know."

"Is that right now. And here I thought all along that it was Santa who did everything himself."

"Nope. Santa has a lot of helpers. He just inspects the toys to make sure they are not broken and then he puts them into a big bag onto his sleigh. And there is a Mrs. Claus too, you know. She feeds Santa cookies and hot chocolate. It is cold all the time where they live, so he needs to be kept warmed up. That is what she does, Dad."

Aaron glanced at his son with amusement in his face. "I see. You seem to have got it all worked out just fine."

Sliding down in his seat, he let out a yep.

"Anything special on your list this year, son?"

Thinking about it, Adam looked at him. "Mom took me to see Santa already, and I asked him if I could have my dad for Christmas. I guess he listened to me."

Aaron's hands gripped the steering wheel, and his eyes teared up. He looked over at Adam who was sitting there so innocently talking about what he wanted for Christmas, not even realizing that things between him and Beth were a little bit more complicated than that. But Aaron promised himself that he would always be there for his son if that is what he wished for.

Christmas was the best day they had ever had. Amy had gone out of her way to add some festive touches to most of the rooms in her house. Not only did Aaron, Laina, and Amy enjoy one another's company, but so did Paula and Adam. Although he didn't have much in the way of toys to play with, Paula kept him fully entertained with her stories and a fun game of hide-and-seek. Although there was still a dark cloud hanging over the women of the house, no one spoke of the one person that was missing from their life. Instead, with smiles on their faces, they raised their wineglasses along with Aaron, making a toast to a future of prosperity, health, and promises of tomorrow.

The days following continued, and now it had stretched into two months, which saw some change. The weather was still dreary looking, but there had been no more snow, and the temperature was slightly warmer than it had been. Aaron had decided to drive down to the lake to breathe the fresh air. Walking along the shoreline, he stopped and picked up a rock and watched as it skipped across the water, creating tiny ripples. He thought about his life up to this point. Beth had gone ahead with the divorce proceedings, and he had already received a copy of the papers. There were no visitation restrictions in regard to his son, but he wished they would move a little closer. Other than that, he was satisfied with the way everything was laid out, and he just needed to get his signature on them and send them back. His mind also drifted to Amy. Over the last while, they had spent a lot of time together and made love whenever there was an opportunity. As for Paula and Adam, they got along exceptionally well, with Paula fitting into the role as big sister. When they were all together, it was like one big happy family. Aaron was crazy about Amy, and he was sure he loved her. She was an amazing woman, and the day that he met her was the best thing that happened. Funny how much life had changed for him since then. For a while after Beth left, he didn't think there would be any more chance of happiness in his life. Pausing for a moment, he watched as a mother duck waddled out of the water followed by her three little ducklings. Stopping, she craned her neck to watch them and waited until they were close behind before moving along. Smiling, he removed his camera from its case and snapped a picture. He never dreamed about how he would like his life to play out; he just waited for the events to unfold for them to be captured. Feeling slightly chilled, he zipped up his jacket and continued on down the rocky path.

CHAPTER 5

S OMETHING WASN'T RIGHT, but she didn't know what. Rolling onto her side, she lay still, not wanting to move until the nausea subsided. Perhaps she was feeling so miserable and exhausted due to the poor nights she had been having of late. Life seemed to have taken on a whole new persona, as if she was performing a role in a play. Her reactions and feelings were far more complex now, and she certainly wasn't the same person she once was a few months ago. Smart and unpredictable, yes. Full of useless distractions and mood swings, no. At work, she felt clumsy and inadequate with the clientele, like she had no real purpose for being there. At the moment, her head hurt like she had been the victim of a bad beating. Rubbing her feet together under the sheets, Amy knew it was nowhere near morning, and all she had done was toss and turn. The half-moon filtered through the window sheers, illuminating the duskiness of the room. Taking a deep breath, she crawled out of bed and dragged her body to the bathroom. Letting the warm tap water run for a few seconds, she splashed her face and pulled on a fleece robe. Letting herself out the back door, she sat on the porch steps, taking in the cool night air. In the distance, she could hear an owl's hoot, loudly communicating its needs. A dog barked. All was still. Nothing moved. She swore the tree a few feet away was silently watching her. She shivered, not sure if it was from the cold or the eerie sensation that engulfed her. Not wanting to catch a chill, she entered the house and settled back into bed.

Over the next few days, Amy felt wretched. Sitting on a stool, she waited for the queasiness to pass. Dee quietly approached and put her hand on Amy's shoulder. "Feeling better?"

"God, no. I feel like I am going to die."

"Here. I brought you some herbal tea. It may help."

"Thank you."

"No need. Listen, honey, I've been concerned about you. Don't you think it's about time you made an appointment to see your doctor?"

Lifting her head up, she looked at Dee. "No need to worry. It is more than likely anxiety, stress, and everything else that goes with it."

"Since when did you become a pro on diagnosing, huh? Quit dancing around the subject. You have some time right now, so it's as good a time as any to make that appointment."

Amy picked up the receiver and dialed the number. "Doctor's office. Can I help you?"

"Um, yes. I would like to make an appointment please."

"Let's see. I have tomorrow at four o'clock. Would that work?"

"Yes, that is fine."

"Could I have your name please?"

"It's Amy. Amy Munro."

"All right, Amy. We'll see you tomorrow at four."

For almost the end of February, it was extremely cold, Amy thought as she climbed into the waiting taxi. Bundled up in a coat and scarf, she made her way to the doctor's office.

She didn't have long to wait before Dr. Mackenzie walked into the room and sat down at her desk. "Hi, Amy. What can I do for you today?"

"Well, for starters, I haven't been feeling myself lately. I feel nauseous at times."

"I see. Is there any particular time that this comes on?"

"No, not exactly. It is more intermittent."

"How is your appetite?"

"Lately I have been picking at my food. I mean, I do eat, but not in abundance."

"Are you still working, Amy?"

"Yes."

"And how is that going?"

"Well, I struggle sometimes with feeling ill and sluggish, but thank goodness, my boss is so understanding."

"So you would say that the symptoms you are experiencing are affecting your job?"

"Yes, I would definitely say that."

"I see. Are you sexually active, Amy?"

"Um, yes. I have been seeing a wonderful man, I guess for about four months now."

"Have you missed your period at all?"

"Yes, I did, but you know, with me I am not always regular anyways."

"I know. Are you still taking birth control pills?"

"Yes, I have been. I had stopped taking them when Nick left but started taking them again since being intimate with Aaron."

"Okay. What we are going to do is start with a urine sample. I'll get you to go down the hall to the washroom, and I will bring you a sterile container. When you are finished, just leave it on the counter in the bathroom and head on back in here. Then what I would like you to do is remove your clothing from the waist down and cover up here on the exam table. Any questions?"

"No."

"Good. Off we go then, and I will see you back here shortly."

When Dr. Mackenzie came back into the room, she quickly examined Amy. "Blood pressure is normal. Okay, Amy. I will pull the curtain, and you can get yourself up, and then we will chat."

Quickly getting dressed, Amy opened the curtain and sat on the chair across from the doctor, waiting for her to speak.

Taking off her glasses, she laid them on her desk and leaned back in her chair. "Well, from what I can tell, you are pregnant. I suspect you are approximately six weeks along."

Amy stared at her dumbfounded. "Are . . . are you sure?"

"Absolutely positive and probably October."

Biting her lip, she looked at Dr. Mackenzie. "How could this have happened? I mean, wow."

"I know it is a shock to you, and the pill is an effective form of birth control. However, even if you miss a day, it increases your chances of getting pregnant. Amy, no form of birth control will prevent pregnancy all the time. Really, the only way to ever make sure it doesn't happen is to not have sex at all. You are planning on keeping the baby?"

"Yes, absolutely. I am not sure how Aaron is going to take it though."

"Hopefully it will all work out for the best. One thing you don't need is any added stress. I would like to see you back in my office in about a month's time, unless of course you need to see me before then."

Amy left the doctor's office confused and close to tears. She wondered how Aaron was going to react when she broke the news to him, and she was in no hurry to do that.

No sooner had Amy arrived at work the next morning than Dee asked how her doctor's appointment went. Amy hadn't even thought about what she was going to say as she had not told anyone at all about her condition. The reality of it was that Dee was going to find out sooner or later as she couldn't hide an expanding abdomen. Hanging up her coat and scarf, she sat down.

"What I am going to tell you goes no further than us for now. I haven't even mentioned it to Aaron yet."

"You haven't told him because why?"

"It's kind of complicated."

"Okay. I'm listening."

"I am pregnant, Dee."

"Oh my. You're sure?"

"Yes. Very sure."

"What are you going to do?"

"Well, I have to first get up enough courage to tell Aaron. From there, it all depends on how he takes it."

"When *are* you going to tell him?"

Amy let out her breath. "To tell you the truth, Dee, I don't know. I can't keep the secret for too long though, because I will eventually start to show."

"Wow. You are in a pickle, aren't you, dear?"

"To say the least. Aaron and I have never discussed the possibility of a child. I mean, maybe he doesn't want any more in his life."

Leaning over, Dee touched Amy's arm. "Somehow he doesn't strike me as that sort. If I can help out in any way, just let me know."

"Thank you." Looking at her watch, she got up. "I guess I should get to work. Time to open up."

As the following week flowed into March, Amy became increasingly restless during the night. She suffered with fatigue and nausea during the day, which made it tougher on her at work. And she still had not told Aaron that she was carrying his child.

Today was not any different than any other morning lately. Sitting in the living room with her feet curled up on a chair, she sat nibbling on soda crackers to help settle her stomach. The curtains were drawn to block out the little bit of sunlight that was shining through the window. Her head hurt, and she was sure her eyes had dark circles under them, but she didn't care. The way she was feeling, she could stay there all day and not move. Reaching for her glass of apple juice, she washed down the dry crackers that she was trying to swallow and knew she had to figure things out right quick like. Hearing footsteps, she lifted her head to find Paula coming to join her.

"Hi there, kiddo."

"Good morning, Mom." Picking up the remote control, she turned on the television and flopped onto the couch.

Amy sat looking at her in thought. For a girl so young, she was very mature for her age. Dressed in jeans and a sweatshirt, her long brown hair was hanging loosely around her shoulders. With the light on her hair, you could see just a hint of copper flecks. Paula was slender in build, but not all that tall, for she had gotten her height from her. From her father came the inherited looks-having the enticing pouty lip, a perfectly formed oval face, and huge hazel eyes. She was lucky as neither her nose was covered in freckles, nor was her face marked in any way. Paula was what you would call an attractive girl and had the personality to go with it. Even though having been an only child, she was never raised to be a spoiled brat. Her manners were impeccable, and she was always well behaved. Amy was proud of the daughter she had raised, and the two of them shared a close, loving bond.

Amy stood at the kitchen window watching the birds at the feeder all trying to be the first to get the seeds. Some were fluttering around in the birdbath. She was trying to cook breakfast for Paula. The bacon was sizzling away in the pan, and she still had the eggs to do. Hearing the doorbell, she called to Paula to answer it; but after a moment of silence, she put her head down and moaned. She knew her voice had gone unheard. Turning the frying pan down, she made her way to the front door and was surprised to see Aaron. After kissing her on the cheek, he walked past her and took off his jacket.

"I should have probably called first, but I was in the neighborhood, so to speak. Figured you'd be up anyways." Walking over to her, he took her in his arms and hugged her. Amy couldn't help thinking how wonderful it felt to be nestled against him.

"It's all right. I am up and cooking breakfast. Can I get you anything?"

"No, thank you. I had breakfast not that long ago, so I'm fine."

"How about a coffee then?"

"Thanks, but no. I have had my fill of that too."

Just then Paula came bounding down the stairs and stopped when she saw Aaron.

"Good morning, Paula."

"Morning, Aaron. How come you are here at this time of the day?"

Amy looked at her daughter and narrowed her eyes. "Paula, you shouldn't be asking questions like that."

"Sorry, but he is never here this early. Just wonderin', that's all."

Aaron winked at her then turned to Amy. "It is all right, and an explanation will be forthcoming." The aroma of the bacon reminded Amy that she had to get back into the kitchen. Paula and Aaron sat down at the table while Amy continued on.

Removing the bacon from the pan, she opened up the fridge door. "How may eggs would you like, Paula?"

"Two please."

Grabbing them, she put them on the counter as she wiped the grease from the pan. After cracking one egg into the pan, she reached for the other egg and swore when it hit the floor with a smack. Grabbing a wet cloth, she got down on her hands and knees and tried to clean up the sloppy mess.

"I just can't believe this. That was really careless of me. One thing I hate is cleaning up slimy eggs off the floor, shell and all." Rinsing the cloth in the sink, she carried on with her tirade. "Of all the stupid things to do. It was my own fault. You cannot put an egg on the counter and expect it to just stay there." Throwing the cloth in the sink, she grabbed the flipper and turned the egg over in the pan and then cursed under her breath when the yolk broke. Aaron and Paula looked at each other with puzzled expressions on their faces. Getting up, he walked over to Amy and took her in his arms.

"What is going on with you?"

With tears forming in her eyes, she sniffled. "I can't seem to do anything right this morning."

"Amy. Take it easy. Things happen."

"No, things happen to me. I can't even seem to cook an egg properly."

Paula wondered why her mom had gotten so uptight. "Mom, it's no big deal. I will eat it anyways. You don't have to make me two."

Still leaning against Aaron's chest, she wiped her eyes. "No, it is okay. You asked for two eggs, and I can throw in another."

"I don't want two, Mom. The one egg and bacon is fine." Getting up, Paula got her breakfast and ate it quite hastily. Putting her plate in the sink, she glanced at her mom with a worried expression and then left the kitchen.

Moving away from Aaron, Amy blew her nose and then started to clean up the kitchen, banging pans as she went. Clearing his throat, he came up behind her and spun her around.

"What on earth has gotten into you? Do you want to sit down and tell me about it?"

"No."

"Is something bothering you, Amy? Is it me? Did I do something to upset you at all?"

"No. It's not you. Just having a rough day is all. I'll be okay."

"Well, there was a reason why I came over this morning. Maybe my news will cheer you up."

Taking her hand, they sat at the table, and she waited for him to continue. He was looking at her with a smile on his face. "You know the kids have spring break soon." She nodded.

"Well, I applied for time off at work and got it. I thought maybe we could all use a vacation. So . . . how would you and Paula like to go to Hawaii with Adam and I?"

"What? You aren't serious!"

"I am very serious. So what do you say?" Putting her head in her hands, he could hear her sigh. This wasn't the reaction he was expecting from her, and he waited for her to speak.

"Aaron, I cannot go to Hawaii. It's impossible. I have my job and . . . oh boy."

"Amy, I am sure if you asked Dee for a week off, she would give it to you. Don't you think?"

"I'm not sure. She might, but that is not the only issue. I don't know if Paula is going to spend the week with her father, or what. We haven't talked about it yet."

Taking her hand, he looked into her eyes. "Okay. So we ask her. You're making it all sound more difficult than it really is."

Getting up, she walked over to the counter and leaned against it. There was no way she could go to Hawaii with him in her condition. "Aaron, I just cannot go. The timing is not good."

"Why? Why is it so hard for you to accept my invitation? You don't have to make it this difficult."

Amy was furious with him. "How dare you imply that I am being difficult! You have no idea . . . You cannot just waltz in here expecting Paula and me to pack up and run off to Hawaii with you."

"Look, the only thing I was expecting from you was a little bit more cooperation, but it seems you are not interested in spending that time with me. Maybe it was a bad idea." Getting up, he pushed in his chair and started to walk out of the kitchen. With her lip quivering, tears started to roll down her cheeks. "Where are you going, Aaron?" Hearing the sob in her voice, he turned around and put his hands in his pants pocket. "I thought it would be best if I left. Hey, I'm sorry. I didn't mean to upset you. I thought it would be a nice break for all of us." Amy started to cry uncontrollably. Now really concerned, Aaron walked over and pulled her into his arms and stroked her hair. "Hey. What is it?"

Her voice quivered. "I . . . I can't t-tell you."

"You can't tell me what?" Choking back the sobs, she shook her head. "Amy, look at me. What can't you tell me?" Lifting her chin with his finger, he stared into her eyes and spoke to her softly. "Tell me."

"Oh, Aaron, I . . . I'm preg-pregnant." The shocked look on his face was enough to get her crying again. He was speechless.

"*What?* Oh, Amy. Are you sure? How do you know?"

"I hadn't been feeling well, so I saw my doctor about two weeks ago, and she confirmed it."

Letting out his breath, he moved away from her and paced. "So you have known for a couple of weeks and didn't even think to tell me that I am going to be a father? Is that why you don't want to go on this trip?"

She nodded. "I didn't tell you because I was afraid to, and I didn't know how you would take the news. Believe me, I never expected this to happen."

"Neither did I, but it has. Does Paula know?"

"No. I haven't told anyone except Dee. So are you angry?"

"Should I be?"

"I don't know. A child means a lifetime of commitment, and maybe it is something you don't want to get involved with again."

"I am hurt that you would think such a thing of me."

Seeing the look in her eyes, he walked over to her and gathered her in his arms and kissed her. "No, love. The only thing I am angry about is that you didn't tell me a lot sooner. I am shocked, but nonetheless pleased." He chuckled. "I cannot believe it. After nine years. Hey, when am I going to be a father again?"

"Oh, the doctor says October."

"October, huh?"

"Uh-huh."

"Well, if the baby isn't due until then, we could still go to Hawaii."

She looked at him in horror. "Nope. Still not a good idea unless you want to take the chance of me getting sick on the plane."

It dawned on him what she was talking about. "Ah, you are suffering with pregnancy sickness."

"Yes, and it is called morning sickness, although I cannot really figure out why it is called that when I suffer off and on throughout the day as well."

"When is your next doctor's appointment?"

"In a week. Why?"

"Because I would like to go with you. I want to be as involved with the baby as you are. When Beth was pregnant with Adam, I was with her throughout every appointment, and I want to be there for you as well."

"What are we going to do? I mean, you are okay with this?"

"I am more than okay with it. Everything is going to work out just fine. We will talk more, but for now I think we have had enough excitement for one day. Don't you agree?"

"Yes. I think you are right."

"Let's leave the Hawaii trip for the time being. There is one other thing that I want to tell you though."

"What?"

"I love you, and I have for a long time."

"Oh, Aaron. That scares me. Nick loved me once too."

"Amy, I am *not* Nick. You have to let it go. It is about me loving you now."

With that, she wrapped her arms around his neck and kissed him passionately.

CHAPTER 6

"**W**HAT DO YOU *mean* you're having a baby? You are in your thirties. What are my friends going to think? Oh my gosh, this is sooo embarrassing." Paula looked like a startled doe, not quite sure if she should stay or run for the hills.

Amy hadn't counted on getting a reaction like that. "So what if I am in my thirties? I kind of hoped you'd be pleased at the thought of having a little brother or sister."

"Mom. Think about it. I am almost thirteen, and I never thought you would have another baby, especially now. You are like a . . . a fossil."

"Excuse me? A fossil? Just what does that mean exactly?"

"It *means* you are getting old. As in look at how old I am and how old you are."

Aaron couldn't hide his laughter. Amy tossed him an amused look. "What the heck is so funny?"

"Just the thought of imagining you as a fossil."

"Paula, where do you possibly come up with these things? I am *not* old, and besides, age has nothing to do with it. There are women who have babies in their late forties, for crying out loud."

"Eww, Mom. This just isn't cool. I thought it would always be just you and me."

"Is this really what the conversation is about? Paula, listen. There is no reason for you to be jealous of this baby if that is the way you are feeling. This is unexpected, yes, but it isn't going to change how I feel about you. Don't forget, Aaron has Adam too. This baby is special because it is not just *mine*. It is everyone's baby."

"I don't know what to say. It is weird thinking about you being pregnant."

Aaron leaned against the wall with his arms folded across his chest. He hadn't told Adam yet but hoped it went in a lot better direction than this conversation was going.

"Yes, I imagine it is. However, you and I could have fun shopping together. I got rid of all your baby stuff ages ago, thinking I wasn't going to have any more. Little did I know."

"I don't want to talk about it anymore right now. I'm going to go to my room."

Letting out her breath, she looked at Aaron. "Okay, fine. I just had an idea though. The tension is very powerful in here, and I feel like I may be electrocuted if I stay here much longer. How about we get out of here for a while."

"I don't know. What did you have in mind?"

"Nothing specific. Let's just be spontaneous and have some fun. I would like to spend some time together. I don't think it is a good idea for you to just take off to your room and hide for the rest of the day."

"Okay. Fine. I'll go."

"Great. Now if Aaron doesn't have any plans, perhaps he would like to make it a threesome."

Amy hugged her daughter. "I love you, you know. Now go get ready because I would like to leave in the next twenty minutes."

"I love you too. Be right back."

Aaron unfolded his arms and walked over to Amy. "Wow, that was explosive."

"Ya, tell me about it. So do you want to come out and play with us?"

"I am slightly tempted. Maybe I could be more persuaded?"

"How about a kiss?"

"That would do it."

"Well then, pucker up." With that, they kissed with a passion two people experience, knowing a new life was created from a shared love.

Amy was tense and exhausted. Stripping out of her clothes, she climbed into the tub. The scent of the vanilla bubble bath was inviting as she slid right down. Laying her head back, she closed her eyes and scooped the bubbles up around her chest and neck. Thinking about her daughter, she wondered if she would eventually be more accepting of her pregnancy. She still hadn't told her mother yet either. Getting out of the tub, she wrapped a towel around herself and got ready for bed. Glancing at the time, she wondered if her mother would still be up and decided to give her a call. Laina picked up on the third ring.

"Hi, Mom."

"Hello, dear. How are you?"

"Tired. Paula, Aaron, and I were out for most of the afternoon. I just got out of the bath, and I am now ready for bed."

"Certainly was a nice day to be out and about."

"Yes, it was. Anyways, Mom, I am calling you because I have some news for you."

"Oh? Good or bad?"

"Well, I would hope you would take it as good news." Amy let her breath out slowly. "Mom, I am pregnant."

There was silence on the other end of the phone, and Amy waited for her to say something. Anything. "That was news I wasn't expecting. Wow. Another grandchild. I gather Aaron is the father?"

"Yes. He is."

"Well, I must say, as much as I am shocked, I am thrilled."

"I kind of thought you would be, Mom."

"So when is the baby due?"

"Early autumn."

"Did you tell Paula yet?"

"Yes, and she didn't exactly jump for joy."

Laina sighed. "Well, you know, dear, she is used to being an only child. She'll come around. Give her some time."

"I suppose. Anyways, I hate to call and run, but I am ready to call it a night. My energy is tapped right out."

"All right, dear. Take good care of yourself. After all, that is my grandchild you are carrying."

Amy laughed. "I know. Good-bye, Mom."

"Night, dear."

After hanging up, Amy pulled back the covers, crawled into bed, and laid her hand on her stomach. It wasn't long before she fell into a dreamless sleep.

Aaron sat back in his office chair twiddling his thumbs. Although he was staring at nothing in particular, his thoughts revolved around the fact that he was going to be a father again. He was excited, but the news certainly threw him for a loop. His divorce from Beth was not yet final, and adding to his family in that manner hadn't entered into his mind. Life was again changing for him, and he would have to make some plans with Amy in regard to their future. He meant it though when he told her he wanted to be involved as much as possible during her pregnancy, and with the baby once it was born. He loved Amy and knew he wanted her and Paula to be a part of his life. So far, he hadn't told Adam about the baby, but that was something he didn't want to do over the telephone. Glancing at his watch, he realized it was time for him to meet Amy at the doctor's for her first prenatal appointment. Putting some papers inside his briefcase, he snapped it shut, put on his jacket, and left the office.

The weather was warming up slightly, but there was still a slight chill in the air as Aaron stepped outside onto the busy street. He decided to leave his car parked and walk. Drivers were honking their horns trying to get things moving a little quicker, and a cabdriver yelled profanities as a cyclist cut in front of him just as the traffic light turned yellow. Hurrying through the door and down the hallway, he looked for Dr. Mackenzie's office. Amy was flipping through a magazine when he sat down next to her. Leaning over, she kissed him and smiled. "You made it."

"Of course. I told you I would be here."

"I know, but I was worried you would get stuck in a meeting or something."

"Not a chance. I made sure Nancy didn't schedule any for today." Just as Amy was going to respond, the receptionist opened the door and told her she could come in now. It wasn't long before Dr. Mackenzie walked in and put her chart on the desk.

"Hi, Amy. How have you been feeling?"

"Lots of morning sickness and tired a lot."

Smiling, the doctor nodded her head. "It'll pass. Hop up here on the bed and let's check you out." She felt around Amy's tummy and listened for the sounds of a heartbeat.

"Do you hear anything, Dr. Mackenzie?"

She shook her head. "It may be too early yet. I was thinking you are about nine to eleven weeks, but you may be just past the two months rather than closer to three months along. No worries though. We will have another listen on your second prenatal visit. I'll just get you to sit up so that I can check your blood pressure, and then I want to get another urine sample from you. Bring a first morning with you for now on if you can remember." Amy nodded.

Amy had just come in from working in the flower beds all day. She had decided to purchase some gardening magazines and see what she could do with the overgrown weeds around the house. From the looks of things, it had been a long time since the soil had been worked and planted. Now petunias and periwinkle graced the yard, but there was much more to be done. For now, she was calling it a day. Dee wasn't kidding when she said it was a lot of hard work, and she didn't feel the rush and excitement as others did working outside. It was more like a tedious chore. Her back was aching, and she was stiff. Her hands were sorely blistered, and she wished she had owned a pair of gardening gloves. Rubbing her palm over her itchy nose, she walked into the kitchen to find Paula eating a bowl of ice cream. Breaking into a giggle, she put her spoon down. Amy raised her eyebrows with a questioning look.

"Mom, you have dirt on your nose."

Washing her hands in the kitchen sink, she grabbed a clean cloth, wiped her nose, and turned to toward Paula.

"Better?"

"Yep. Much."

Just as Amy was about to sit down, the phone rang. Answering it, she was surprised to hear Nick's voice on the other end.

"Amy? It's Nick."

"Hi, did you want to speak to Paula?"

"For the moment, no. I wanted to speak to you actually."

"Oh? What about?"

"I was talking to Paula yesterday. I understand you are expecting a baby. Congratulations."

Stunned, she did not know what to say.

"Hello? Are you still there?"

"Ah, yes, Nick, I am. Sorry. You kinda caught me off guard."

"I wanted to talk to you about our marriage. We have been separated now for a few months. I was thinking one of us should file for a divorce."

Amy's mouth dropped open. "What do you mean one of us?"

Nick hesitated. "Well, I was thinking that since you have a baby on the way, and I am involved with someone else, it was about time to dissolve our marriage. Don't you think?"

"What do I think? I think that if you want a divorce, you file. You were the one that left me. Remember? Besides, you're the high-class lawyer."

"Amy, you don't have to get so snappy."

"I have every right to be snappy, Nick. You broke up a family. You left, and I had to look for a job with the only skills I had so that I could support our daughter. I work in a florist shop, for crying out loud. Now you phone me when I am in the first trimester of my pregnancy and 'suggest' that one of us should file for a divorce. What kind of shit is that?"

"Would you rather stay married then?"

"You know what, Nick? I didn't stop to think about what to do about our marriage because I was too busy picking up the pieces. Plus I have had a lot on my plate lately, so to speak. Couldn't this have even waited for a little while longer? Did you ask what I thought when you were planning on walking out the door? No, you didn't. You just up and left, and you have no idea what that did to me, emotionally. I bet you never lost any sleep."

"Look, I understand that you are bitter and hurt, and I didn't expect it to be easy on you when I left. But the point is, I just think that we both need to carry on with our lives."

Amy started to cry softly into the phone. "Just who needs to carry on with their lives, Nick. You or me? Somehow I am guessing this conversation is all about you, because it always was."

Letting his breath out slowly, he remained silent for a moment. "I didn't call to get into an argument with you or have you beat me up over the phone."

"What did you expect? That this was going to be a hunky-dory conversation, and I'd invite you over so that we could talk about this happily over coffee?"

"No, I didn't expect that at all. For whatever it is worth, Amy, I don't ever regret marrying you or having our daughter. I just fell out of love with you. That's all."

Sniffling, Amy reached over and took a Kleenex out of the box and blew her nose. "I need to go, Nick. Just start the divorce if you want to. I wouldn't take you back anyways if I was paid a million dollars. Do you want to talk to Paula now?"

"Yes, put her on. Take care of yourself."

Amy handed the phone over and walked out of the kitchen and up the stairs. Walking down the hallway to her bedroom, her head began to swim, and the walls seemed to be closing in on her. She could feel her heart beating rapidly, and gasping for breath, she took her medication and then curled up on the bed. She wept for the life that she once had, the love that she had lost, and the future that lay ahead.

Just as the morning light was coming through the windows, Amy awoke feeling quite ill. Not moving, she swallowed hard, hoping it would go away. It wasn't long before she scrambled out of bed and ran for the bathroom. With head bent over the toilet, she heaved, hoping it would stop as suddenly as it came on. She felt clammy and started to shake. It was bad enough that her stomach hurt from the early morning retch. Flushing the toilet, she turned on the cold water and rinsed her mouth. She felt lousy and hoped she would not have to endure this for too much longer. Knowing she would not be able to sleep, she went down the stairs and curled up in her favorite cozy living room chair. Wrapping a blanket around her shoulders, there was no sound except the *tick, tick,* ticking of the clock sitting on top of the fireplace mantle. Turning on the table lamp beside her, she picked up her book and attempted to read it but couldn't seem to get past the first page. Slamming it shut, she rubbed her eyes and went out into the kitchen. Making herself tea, she slowly sipped away at it, waiting for the opportunity to give

Dee a call. Amy knew for certain that she would not be going into work that day and thought she may even have to think about cutting her hours back some. She didn't know how Dee would feel about that though as right now the two of them were a team, and most days they found themselves busy. Probably hiring another part-time girl would be out of the question, but something would have to be worked out. She was startled suddenly by the sound of two outside cats fighting and put her hand to her chest. Her heart was racing, and she was feeling a little jumpy. Glancing at the time, she got up and dialed Dee's number, knowing she would be up, and then made herself some toast with jam.

With the phone pressed to his ear and resting on his shoulder, Aaron picked up his pen and doodled on the notepad in front of him. With a scowl on his face, he listened as Beth spoke. He was wanting to have Adam all of next week, but she was not being very cooperative.

"Listen, Beth, you are just making excuses, as far as I am concerned, and I don't know why."

"It is not my fault that my sister and her family are coming to visit."

"You've never stopped me from taking him before, so why now? Your sister and her family do not come first. I do. Did you even think to ask him what he'd rather do?"

"No, I didn't. My sister hasn't seen Adam for almost a year and a half. I kind of went with the family plans."

"Well, to hell with your family plans." Throwing his pen across the desk, he watched as a piece of paper slid off and floated to the floor.

"Don't you dare use that kind of tone with me, Aaron."

"Well then, don't stop me from spending time with my son. Why don't you just be fair about it all and ask him to decide. I don't want to have to take you to court to work out permanent visitation, but if I have to –"

"Are you threatening me?"

"No, not in the least. It is fact. Bottom line is, when you wanted the divorce, it was agreed that I could see Adam when I wanted to. Now, I am not allowed."

Sighing, she was silent on the other end.

"Beth, you cannot keep Adam from me. You have to know that I am not going to allow that to happen without a fight first."

"All right. Fine. When I get off the phone, I will go and talk to him about it."

"No, I think you should call him right now and ask so I can hear what he has to say, without any persuasion on your part."

"Aaron, I resent that."

"Look, if I have to, I will sit here all night with you, but I would much rather just get it settled right away. Could you just call him and ask please?"

Putting the phone down, Beth called to Adam while Aaron waited on the other end. When she picked up again, he could hear his son in the background.

"Okay, he is here, and I will ask him. Adam, remember I told you that Aunt Shalane, Uncle Lee, and the kids are coming next week?"

"Uh-huh."

"Well, Daddy is on the phone and wants to know if you could spend next week with him. What do you say?"

Screwing up his face, he thought about it. "I want to see Daddy, but I want to have a sleepover with Matt and Kevin too."

She didn't think that was going to happen. "Adam, they will be here on Saturday, so how about having a sleepover that night and then going with your dad the next day for the rest of the week? That way, you get to do both. How does that sound?"

"It sounds okay."

"Give me a moment, honey, so I can ask your dad if he is agreeable with that."

"Aaron, would that arrangement satisfy you?"

"It is not me we have to satisfy here. It is our son. If it works for him, it works for me. Can I talk to him?"

"Yes, of course. I guess you and I are finished now?"

"We are. And, Beth, next time, don't try this on me. You are just going to make things harder on yourself than what they need to be."

With a touch of hostility in her voice, she said good-bye and handed Adam the phone.

"Hi, Dad."

"Hey there. So next week you and I are gonna hang out. That is pretty exciting, eh?"

"Ya. Cool, and I get to see my cousins too. We like to pretend we are camping out at night all by ourselves."

Aaron chuckled. "That sounds like fun. Can anybody come?"

"Nope. No parents allowed. Just kids."

"Ah. I see. Well, have fun on your campout. I will be there on Sunday to pick you up. Probably around noonish. We'll stop along the way for lunch like we normally do."

"Okay."

"See you soon, Adam."

"Yep. Bye, Dad."

Hanging up the receiver, the conversation he just had with Beth was still on his mind. He didn't mean to lose his temper with her, but he had to prove once and for all that when it came to his son, he wasn't going to back down and play second fiddle.

Sliding on a pair of sweatpants and a sweater, Amy walked out the front door into the late morning air. A good, solid walk was what she figured would cure her mood. She was agitated, and home was beginning to feel like a prison. The walls seemed to be closing in on her, no matter which room of the house she was in; and although the windows were free and clear of any bars, she felt trapped. Keeping a fast pace, she looked around her and saw that spring was clearly once again born. Two little girls were standing on their front lawn blowing bubbles into the air, watching as they floated their way up, only to finally disappear. Nearing a tiny park, Amy saw the occasional jogger or cyclist. Although she wasn't sure if her stomach would be able to handle anything, she walked toward the small concession stand. Just the smell of the food made her crave it. Standing in line, she waited her turn.

"What'll it be, ma'am?" asked the vendor.

"I'd like two hot dogs please."

"Grilled onion on that, miss?"

"No. Plain is just fine. Thanks."

Turning around, he yelled the order out to the cook, "Two more hot dogs, Pete. No onion." Looking at Amy, he motioned for her to move to the side so he could take his next order. "Won't be too long."

The young man behind Amy was standing with one hand in his pocket and the other holding a dog leash. "Nice time of the day for a walk, wouldn't you say?"

"It sure is." Eyeing the dog, she noticed how obedient he was, just sitting there panting, waiting for his master's next command. "Can I pet the dog?"

"Oh, sure you can."

Squatting down, she rubbed the top of his head and underneath the chin. "Male or female?"

"Male. Name is Tucker."

"Tucker. What a nice name."

"Miss, your hot dogs are ready," called the vendor.

Taking them, she added a little ketchup and mustard and bit into one.

Tucker sat still, staring at her with a hopeful look in his eye that she was going to either share her food or drop a nibble on the ground. Allowing the leash to fall, the man commanded Tucker to stay while he got his food. Watching him, she mopped up the mustard that dropped on her sleeve.

"What a good boy you are! What breed of a dog is he?"

"Tucker is a harrier. Have you ever heard of them?"

"No. I am not familiar with them at all. But he looks almost like a beagle."

"Yes, he does. The harrier originates from England and is similar to the foxhound, but smaller. They weigh between forty and sixty pounds. Interestingly enough, there is a couple of conflicting stories as to their origin. One is that the earliest harrier types were crossed with bloodhounds, the basset hound, and the Talbot hound while the other side being that the breed was probably developed from crosses of the English foxhound with greyhound and fox terrier. They're very gentle, sociable, playful, and inquisitive dogs. Also very active, and they make a better companion if they are well exercised. They don't make very good apartment dogs, that's for sure. I ended up having to move into a house with a decent backyard, and he'd go out there and dig when I let him out. Had to nip that one in the butt real fast, so now he doesn't do that anymore. We walk this route almost every day, so he knows it well. Sniffs his way through the park, nose to the ground. Don't ya, Tucker." Bending down, he pulled a dog biscuit out of his pocket and gave it to him. Picking up the leash, Tucker stood up and wagged his tail.

"It was nice chatting with you. My name is Nathan, by the way." He extended his hand, and Amy shook it.

"Likewise, and I'm Amy." Kneeling down, she giggled as she felt a wet tongue on her hand. "It was nice to meet you too, Tucker."

"I guess we should get our walk finished. Maybe we will meet up again sometime. Do you come here often?"

"No, just once in a while."

"Okay, well, enjoy your walk."

"You too." Inhaling deeply, she continued on her way, walking briskly almost as if she was being followed, never once stopping. She could feel her adrenaline pumping, and by the time she got home, she flopped onto her back on the sofa. Exhausted, she thought about the two new friends she had just made.

CHAPTER 7

S TEPPING INTO THE lobby of the hotel, Amy looked around. It was crowded, and not seeing Nick, she settled into a seat to avoid being jostled. Selecting a magazine off the table, she flipped through the pages, tapping her foot impatiently. He had called and asked if she would meet him for dinner so they could go over the divorce papers that were drafted up. Not that she wanted to be here, but she knew it was best to get things over and done with for everyone's sake. Just as she was wondering if he was going to be much longer, he came through the revolving doors almost at a run. His disheveled hair and facial lines told her his day had been a long, tiring one. Laying the magazine down, she stood up with a cold look on her face. Leaning over to kiss her cheek, she quickly turned away and walked just slightly behind him as they entered the restaurant. Since Nick was a regular patron, they were shown immediately to a table for two. Handing them each a menu, the waiter stood with his hands behind his back.

"Could I get either of you anything to drink from the bar?"

Shaking her head, she glanced at the menu. "I will just have an iced tea please, with a wedge of lemon."

"Certainly, ma'am. And for you, sir?"

"A scotch please."

"I will be right back with your drinks."

Snapping open his briefcase, Nick pulled out some papers and laid them on the table. "You are looking a little tired. Feeling okay?"

"I'm fine. Thank you for asking."

"How is Paula?"

"Doing great. She got her report card and, as always, straight As and Bs across the board."

"That is fantastic, but I'm not surprised in the least. Always was a good student."

"Yes, she has been. However, I had wondered if her grades would be affected at all when you left."

The waiter appeared with their drinks and asked if they were ready to order. Nick looked across at Amy, and she nodded.

"I am going to have a spinach salad. I don't have a huge appetite tonight."

"Fine. I will have a steak please, medium rare with baked potato and a green salad to start."

"Thank you." With that, the waiter removed the menus and left.

Loosening his tie and unbuttoning his suit jacket, he picked up his drink and leaned back in his chair. "So would you prefer to look over the papers now, or after we have eaten?"

"I think we should leave it until after we'd eaten. Otherwise, my dinner may go untouched. That would be such a waste of your money, don't you think?"

"Touché. Amy, either we can try to be civil, which would make for a much less stressful evening, or we can sit here and bash each other. It's up to you, but I would much rather get along."

"I just want to get through this as fast as possible and leave here without being a nervous wreck."

As they ate, Nick tried to carry on a conversation while Amy was not very subtle at showing her lack of enthusiasm. To others, she looked like the average patron; but for her, she was only going through the motions. Nick was definitely getting irritated. "Amy, I'd really appreciate it if you'd stop treating me like I was invisible."

"I'd prefer to think that you're more of an illusion than invisible. You see, that way, I know the person who appears to be sitting across from me is actually false."

"That is enough."

"Oh, but I'm not finished yet."

"I think you are."

"My impression of what reality stood for was eventually shattered by a false deception. The dreams I had, well, they became illusive to me. I cannot get them back because there is no place for them now." Amy's eyes started to well up with tears.

"Amy, stop making me out to be the devil incarnate."

A formation of questions popped into Amy's head. "Nick, how could you just up and leave a family like that? Just pass us off like yesterday's garbage and walk away?"

"I guess marriage revealed something about me. As much as I tried to make myself believe that I was happy with my life, I wasn't. Somewhere along the path, I lost it. The fishing line got tangled so bad that I couldn't unravel it enough to save it. So I chose to just cut the line, let it go, and move on. Morally, it was the right thing, but I know the principle of it all stinks. There aren't enough words or ways to make you understand. I'm sorry."

"You can apologize and justify your actions until the cows come home if that is going to give you a clear conscience, but that is all it is going to accomplish. There is nothing you could ever say to me that would make my feelings change. I don't know if it is hate or pity that I have for you. However, now that old wounds are festering, let's just cut to the chase and get down to the reason why we are actually here." After the table was cleared of dishes, they proceeded to go over the papers.

Putting on his glasses, Nick moved his chair closer to Amy's. "I have kept things as simple as possible, and there is not really much in regard to the division of assets. Paula can continue to reside with you if she wishes, but we will share joint custody. I will continue to pay you the same amount of child support every month until she is moved out and on her own. If she continues on to college or university, I can take care of the expenses. That is not a problem. For what is in the accounts now, I can pay you out half of everything; and when the house sells, you will get half of that as well. Is there anything that you don't agree with at all?"

"No, I think it all sounds reasonable. Have you listed the house yet?"

"Yes, but there has been no offers yet."

"I would like you to give me at least a day or two to think this over before signing the papers though."

Removing his glasses, he looked at her. "Why?"

"Well, just because I think it seems to be satisfactory, I would still like to have a lawyer look it over. I would just like a little time, and I do have that right."

"If you insist. I will leave you with a copy, and just let me know when you have things in order."

As they left, he offered to give her a lift home.

"No, thanks. I will just call a cab and be on my way."

"Listen, Amy. For all its worth, I still care very much for you. I don't want to see you walking away with nothing but bitterness." Taking a chance, he moved closer and put his arms around her. "I am glad you showed up tonight. Are you sure I cannot give you a ride?"

"I'm sure."

Hugging each other, Amy felt his lips on her forehead. "Well, good night then."

"Good night, Nick." Almost at the point of hyperventilating, Amy covered her face with her hands and inhaled slow, deep breaths. It was quiet, just the odd headlight shining in her direction.

Sliding her fingers through her hair, she stood, patiently waiting for her ride. Although it was not excessively chilly out, she wrapped her coat tighter around herself and shivered.

The phone rang, and he picked up on the first ring and smiled at the sound of Amy's voice.

"Hi, sweetheart. What's up?"

"I wanted to let you know that I moved my doctor's appointment up by three days. It is tomorrow morning instead."

"Oh? Why?"

"Well, I have been feeling a little crampy and have started spotting slightly. I just want to make sure that the pregnancy is going fine."

"Is there anything to worry about? I mean . . . like is this normal?"

"I'm not sure. I never experienced anything like this when I was pregnant with Paula. The doctor's office felt I should come in a little earlier and see Dr. Mackenzie."

"What time is your appointment tomorrow?"

"Ten thirty. I know it is short notice, but do you think you'll be able to make it?"

"Ah, let's see. I have one appointment scheduled for nine o'clock, but that can be easily changed. I'll get Nancy right on that."

"Okay. I will see you tomorrow."

"Hey, listen. Are you going into work tomorrow?"

"I highly doubt it. Not if I still have these symptoms. I think I would feel a lot better if I was at home keeping off my feet."

"I will come by and pick you up in the morning just shortly after ten."

"Oh, Aaron, you don't have to do that. I can just meet you there."

"Not on your life. I won't come into the office until later on. I'll come by and see you after work tonight though. How about I bring Chinese? That way, you and Paula don't have to cook."

"Hmm. Chinese, huh? Well, you certainly didn't have to twist my arm very far."

"Anything in particular that you would like me to pick up?"

"Nope. Whatever you order is fine with me, except if it's seafood. As far as I'm concerned, those little critters can stay in the water. If you like it, go ahead, but don't order any on my account."

Aaron laughed. "You're one funny lady. I'll see you around six."

"I'll be waiting."

After disconnecting with Amy, he pressed the intercom button and waited for Nancy to answer.

"Yes, Aaron?"

"Nancy, I have a nine o'clock appointment tomorrow morning that I need to change for later on in the day. Preferably midafternoon. If Mr. Reynolds is unable to make it, just rebook when it is convenient for him. Can you take care of that right away for me, please?"

"No problem. I'll make that call right now."

Dr. Mackenzie sat and looked at the both of them. After examining Amy, she still could not pick up the baby's heartbeat, so she had left the room and called over to the hospital.

"I called over to ultrasound, and they are expecting you. At this point, we need to see how far along you are and check the baby. After that, just come right back here, and we will go over the results."

As they left the office, Rosalinde Mackenzie followed with a look of concern on her face.

Aaron sat in the waiting room while Amy was getting checked.

"Ms. Munro? You may come in now."

Glancing around the darkened room, Amy felt sick to her stomach and nervous.

"My name is Keila, and I am going to be doing your ultrasound. So if I could get you to lie up here on the bed. I am also going to get you to pull your gown up past your tummy for me, and then we will just cover you up some with this sheet. Have you ever had an ultrasound before?"

"Yes, long time ago though."

"This is your second pregnancy?"

"Yes."

"All right, just relax. I am going to put some warm gel on your stomach and use this little transducer device so that I can form a picture of the baby on the ultrasound screen. You may feel a little pressure. I will be doing a vaginal ultrasound as well using a wand-shaped probe. I will gently insert it and move it around. This procedure doesn't hurt, but it may feel a little uncomfortable. Do you have any questions at all?"

"Am I going to get to see the baby?"

"At this point, Amy, no. I am just going to do a quick scan, and then I understand that your doctor would like to see you again."

Amy lay there and started to shake through the scan.

"Are you cold? I can certainly get you a blanket out of the warmer if you'd like."

"No, I'm warm enough. I guess it is just nerves."

"I am going to do the vaginal ultrasound now, so just let me know if you need me to stop. Just take a minute to breathe and just try to relax. It is going to feel more along the lines of having a pelvic exam."

It wasn't long before Keila was finished. Switching off the monitor, she looked at Amy.

"I am going to be right back as I want to get one of the doctors here to just have a quick look as well. Then you'll be on your way."

Half an hour later, Amy and Aaron were both back in Dr. Mackenzie's office. Putting on her glasses, she glanced over the report that had just been faxed over.

"The news, I am afraid, is not good. You are about sixteen weeks into your pregnancy. Normally, I would have been able to hear the baby's heartbeat, which was why I sent you over for the ultrasound. Unfortunately, your baby is not alive at this point. I'm sorry."

As the tears welled up in Amy's eyes, Aaron took her hand, and they sat there in silence.

"The baby is a little smaller than it should be at sixteen weeks' gestation. With the spotting and the cramping you are now experiencing, it is quite possible that you would eventually have miscarried it. What I need to do now is get you an appointment right away with a gynecologist. If you don't mind waiting here a minute, I will go and make some calls."

As Dr. Mackenzie left the room, Amy sobbed uncontrollably. Gathering her into his arms, Aaron just held her, not knowing what to say. He was hurting as much as she was.

Reappearing, Dr. Mackenzie touched Amy's shoulder in sympathy.

"Okay. I managed to get you in with Dr. Tamsyn Keith, and she is actually right upstairs on second floor, room 206. You can head right on up there now as she is expecting you. Listen, Amy, I am truly sorry, and I know that there is nothing I can possibly say that will make it any easier. However, you know how to get in touch with me if you need to. Good luck."

Dr. Tamsyn Keith was a petite blonde in her late thirties, very soft spoken, and quite popular for her great bedside manner. Both Aaron and Amy were taken with her immediately. Sitting straight up in her chair, with both hands folded on the desk, she looked across at them.

"What you are going through is what is called a spontaneous abortion, which means that the fetus is no longer living and does not pass out of the uterus. The pregnancy terminates before fetal development has reached twenty weeks. The embryo stops growing, which makes it an immature embryo. A spontaneous abortion is nature's way of terminating something that was not likely to result in a normal delivery."

Amy squeezed Aaron's hand so hard he flinched. Looking at her, her emotions were very stoic. "What I am going to need to do is exam you, Amy. Although the fetus is smaller than what it should be at growth for sixteen weeks, dilating the cervix enough to pass even a twelve-week fetus is difficult. That could mean putting you into labor and having you deliver the fetus. Come step into this room, undress from the waist down, and then cover up on the bed."

Amy looked at Dr. Keith in horror and screamed at her. "Oh my god! Oh nooo! There is *no* way you can expect me to actually deliver this baby. Do you not have a . . . a . . . conscience or something? That is brutality." Facing Amy, she put her hand on her shoulder and stared into her eyes. "I understand fully how affected you are by this, and it's not going to be easy. The first step is to check you out, which will determine how we can proceed. I want you to think of me as your friend, not as your enemy." While Amy was in with the doctor, Aaron sat there with a grim look on his face, not really understanding how something like this could have happened. He knew how he was feeling, and he could only imagine the heartache that Amy was suffering. It wasn't long before she returned, taking a seat beside him and reaching for his hand. Dr. Keith pulled her chair around from behind her desk so that she was sitting in front of them both.

"Since I have examined you, the baby is small enough to be removed without having you go into labor and deliver it. We would do what is called a D & C. What that means is, you would go into surgery, and the baby would be removed vaginally. You would be put to sleep of course."

Reaching for the Kleenex box on her desk, she handed it to Amy, who was crying and inconsolable.

"I know this is a very traumatic experience for you both, but you will be able to conceive again. Your surgery will be done tomorrow, so I will have my receptionist call you later on today with the time. Nothing to eat or drink after midnight, but she will go over all that with you before you leave the office. Do either of you have any questions?"

Amy shook her head, and Aaron remained silent, thinking that there was absolutely nothing that he could possibly ask that would make it all seem better.

Feeling numb and dazed, Amy walked up the stairs to the solitude of her bedroom. Collapsing onto the bed, she cried for the baby that was not meant to be and wondered if she was going to make it through unscathed.

With his hand on the door handle, he started to turn the knob but then changed his mind and tapped softly. Not getting a response, he opened the door and went slowly inside the bedroom. The curtains were pulled across, and the room was void of any light. "Amy?"

Letting out a little moan, she asked, "What are you doing here?"

"Well, for one, I have been feeling like a lost soul for the past week. I have never felt so helpless in my life. Other than that, I was wondering how long you were going to stay retired from reality. The surgery has been done now, and I don't like seeing you like this."

"Like what? A basket case?"

"No. I don't like seeing you living in your bedroom. It's not healthy, you know."

"If you are here to lecture me, I don't want to hear it."

"Sweetheart, I am not here to do that at all. Paula and I are concerned about you. You have been hiding yourself away for the last week, and you need to start getting up and think about going back to work."

"Aaron, I don't want to do anything. When I am sleeping, I don't have to think about anything."

"You are taking the easy way out. Have you seen your doctor at all?"

"No."

"Well, maybe you should."

Swallowing, her mouth was feeling dry, and she closed her eyes to try to stop the tears that were forming. Touching Amy's hair, Aaron swallowed hard.

"Listen, Amy, I know losing the baby has been hard on you, but you need to continue on. You are neglecting the people that care about you and love you the most. Paula needs you, and so do I. Your mother has called and left messages as well, which you haven't bothered to return."

Getting up, he walked over to the window and pulled the curtains, letting in a little bit of sunlight. Startled by the sudden brightness of the room, Amy propped herself up against the pillows and followed Aaron's movements with her eyes. She watched him as he opened up her dresser drawers and pulled out pieces of clothing.

"What are you doing going through my things?"

"I am getting you up and dressed. That is what I am doing."

"You have no right to come in here like this and tell me what I am going to do, when I don't want to do it."

Standing beside the bed, he threw back the covers and lifted her out. Carrying her into the bathroom, he put her down and handed her the clothes he found.

"Now, do whatever it is that you are going to do, but don't leave here until you are dressed."

"I hate you . . . I hate you . . . I hate you." In a huff, she picked up her hairbrush and hurled it his way just as he walked out and slammed the door shut.

Humming away to herself, Amy looked through the rack of dresses. Biting her lip, she wasn't sure if she liked anything that she had seen so far. Aaron had given her some money, insisting that she buy herself something new. It had been awhile since she had been out, and she was finding the shopping expedition to be more frustrating than exciting.

"Pardon me, ma'am. Can I help you find anything in particular?"

Startled, Amy turned around to see a young salesgirl with a measuring tape hanging loosely around her neck.

"No, thank you. I was just browsing."

"Have you found anything so far that you like?"

"Not yet."

"Do you have any particular color or style in mind?"

"No, not really."

Eyeing her up and down, the salesgirl smiled.

"You know, I have this dress that just came in late yesterday afternoon that I haven't had a chance to put out yet. I think it would look very nice on you. If you like, I can show it to you."

"Yes, I'd like to see it."

Amy continued to browse while the girl went to get the dress.

"Here it is." It was sage in color, with spaghetti straps and a short V neckline.

"What do you think?"

"It is nice but maybe a bit fancier than I had in mind."

"Well, why don't you try it on, at least for fun?"

"I suppose I could."

It wasn't long before Amy appeared out of the dressing room and stood in front of the full-length mirror. Glancing at the salesgirl, she waited for her to speak.

"It's absolutely stunning on you. The color suits you as well as the cut of the dress. It gives you a very slimming and defined look. Very chic. What do you think?"

"Green shades are definitely my color, and I love the way it molds my body. The material is nice."

"It is polyester."

"I just wonder if this is a little too fancy. You know what I mean?"

"Well, it's not that it is fancy, just more versatile. It is simply made. However, what makes the dress gorgeous is that you can add accessories and style it up. You can wear it a lot in many different ways."

"I see what you mean. You have me sold."

"Awesome. It really does look stunning on you. I'll wrap it up."

Leaving the store, Amy was relieved that her shopping excursion was over, although it had not taken up very much of her day. She was tired, and that was about all she could handle.

CHAPTER 8

AS THE SCHOOL bus pulled up in front of the house, Paula got off in a sour mood and slowly walked up the path to the front door. She hated coming home as things were the same every day since Amy had lost the baby. Her mother was always shut up in her room and rarely made an appearance. Aaron stopped by often, and as much as he tried, Amy was not easy to deal with by any means. Not only had she changed, but so had Paula, doing as much as she could around the house and barely getting through her schoolwork. She took meals to her mother, but she ate very little and refused the rest. She was a shell of the woman she once was. Her skin was pale, and she was thin from the weight she lost, and she was still dropping. Amy would be naive to think that Paula hadn't noticed, but she had. For such a young girl, she was not so little in years. She knew something was wrong for a long time now, but she couldn't put a name to it. That was because no one ever said. Dropping her school books down on the table, she poured herself a glass of juice and, just as she did every day, walked up the stairs to let her mother know she was home. Knocking on her door, she entered the bedroom and heard noises coming from the bathroom. Peeking in, she saw Amy sitting on the floor with her knees pulled up to her chest, shaking and crying. Still in her pajamas and feet bare, her hair had gone uncombed. Standing where she was without saying a word, she knew her presence had gone undetected. Why was her mother sobbing like a wounded puppy? Never had she seen her in this state before, and it scared her. With a thought, she stepped out and searched through her mom's phone book lying on the night table and, finding Aaron's work number, called him.

"Hi, Paula. I am surprised to hear from you. What can I do for you?"

"I am sorry to call you at work, but I didn't know what to do. It's Mom. She is on the bathroom crying hard."

Aaron let out a sigh and sat there for a moment, thinking.

"Are you able to get her downstairs at all, or at least out of the bathroom?"

"I don't think so."

"All right, just leave her then, but keep an eye out. I will just quickly finish up what I am doing, and then I will be right over."

"Aaron, what is wrong with her? I am really scared."

"She is sad and having a rough time. I know this is tough on you, but just hang in there. I'll see you soon."

"Okay."

Hanging up the phone, Paula sat on Amy's bed and listened to her until Aaron appeared.

Squatting down, Aaron looked at her with concern on his face.

"Amy? What is going on?"

Lifting her tearstained face up, he noticed her eyes were all red and swollen. It was quite obvious that she had been like this for quite some time.

Saying not a word, she stared at him as the tears continued to run down her face and drip onto her already-wet pajama bottoms.

"Amy, listen, you need to get up off the floor. Do you think you can do that for me?"

"I . . . I . . . don't wa-want to. Leave me a-alone."

"Come on, you need to get up. Do you think it is good for Paula to see you like this?"

"Noooo. This isn't good."

"You're right. This isn't good, and you have been like this for some time now. You have to do something about it. I've pretty much had enough of this."

Looking into Amy's eyes, he watched them to see if she was comprehending what he was saying, but she just stared like he wasn't even there. She sat fixed and unmoving.

"Have you even seen your doctor at all?"

Amy nodded.

"How often?"

Shrugging, Amy put her head back down on her knees and mumbled. "Couple times."

"Amy, a couple of times is not going to do it. Have you even told her what has been going on with you?"

"Yes."

"Well, somehow I cannot see your doctor just letting you be like this. Did she say what is wrong with you?"

"Just a lot of stress in my life."

Looking at his watch, he noticed it was getting close to four o'clock.

"What time is your doctor's office open till?"

"Four thirty. Why?"

"Because you are going to get yourself an appointment. You can call either right now or first thing tomorrow morning, but you *will* do it."

"Aaron, I don't want to go to the doctors. I hate having to get up and get dressed just to go out."

"Listen, Amy. I have seen you like this for about three months now or more. I will be here to help you, but you have to want to help yourself first. If you don't, then there is nothing that either I or Paula can do for you. It isn't fair to expect either one of us to pick up the pieces of your life for you, because you don't want to. Do you understand what I am telling you?"

Sniffling, Amy looked at him and nodded.

Aaron continued. "Furthermore, your daughter is only twelve, well, almost thirteen, if you want to be exact; and she has been living her life, plus yours, for the last while. She goes to school, hangs out with her friends, but then what does she have to look forward to once she walks through that door after school? Absolutely nothing.

She comes home to a mother who doesn't even bother to cook dinner or do a lick of housework because you are in bed most of the day or crying. Do you know how Paula even exists? She does the laundry, the cleaning, and the cooking; and she shouldn't have to be. You've got it backward because you should be looking after her, not the other way around. You need to fix that, and only you can be the one to do it."

"I know I am hurting Paula, but I can't help it. I don't want to go to the doctors though. When I wake up in the morning, it feels good just to not have to get dressed and do anything." She was in a dark hole. An abyss. It embraced her and she felt safe. Now he was asking her to leave it, but she wanted to stay. He didn't know or understand.

"You cannot escape from the world, Amy. No matter what, it is always going to be another day, and you need to start facing it. If you make an appointment, I will gladly go with you, but I will tell you this much. If you choose not to, then I refuse to sit here and watch you like this."

"I thought you loved me, Aaron."

"I do and very much. That is why I will not stick around and watch you be like this. My life is worth more to me than this. What enjoyment do you think I get when you don't want to do anything except mope. We don't go out at all because you don't feel like it. It's not the same anymore, Amy, and you had better get yourself straightened out."

"I cannot believe that you would leave, just like that. I mean, you men must be all alike."

She saw his jaw clench and knew she had gotten a reaction. "I am *not* Nick, and you had best remember that. I am going to take Paula out for something to eat. In the meantime, pull yourself together." Without saying anything more, he got up and suddenly left. As he made his way down the hallway, he could hear Amy yelling at him, but he did not bother to stop.

Stepping through the restaurant door and onto the sidewalk after a business luncheon, Aaron couldn't believe how hot it had gotten. It was already the middle of June, and the streets were crowded with tourists and people who wanted to be out enjoying the weather. Whistling, he removed his jacket and, laying it over his arm, walked the short distance back to the office, pleased with the way his day was going. Picking up mail from Nancy on the way into his office, he flipped through the stack and noticed there was something from Beth's lawyer. Kicking the door shut with his foot, he put the rest of the mail on his desk and, picking up the letter opener, slit open the top of the envelope. Reading through, he realized that he was being informed that the divorce between him and Beth was now final. Putting the papers aside, he sat down and, taking a deep breath, did not move for what seemed like hours. Conscious of the time ticking away, he knew he had a lot of work to do yet, but he did not feel like he could even think straight. Although he had had Amy in his life and loved her, he had loved Beth too. Sealing that chapter of his life was a little difficult to do, and the feelings that went through him made it all seem surreal. He and Beth would now be free to carry on with their lives in the manner that they saw fit. Thinking about Amy, he had not seen her for two weeks now. She had called him the day after he had left her house, and she had not made an appointment with Dr. Mackenzie. Since then, she had called on occasion; but he had not picked up, knowing he needed some time to sort things out on his own.

It was dark as Amy stood in the living room with her elbow on the mantle, holding a glass of wine. She went through her days feeling so down and had not been to work at all. Dee had hired on another girl temporarily until she was well enough to come back. If she ever did. For a long time, she had been feeling like life was hopeless, and her perspectives had changed. Most of her life, she could never understand how people could end their own lives over issues that they were not capable of handling. She figured that nothing could ever have been so bad. Now, at this point in her life, she knew why and was certain she was feeling what every one of them had at the time. Closing her eyes, she wondered if she reopened them if she would disappear to some other place rather than where she was. Raising the glass to her lips, she emptied its contents and then threw it across the room. She had no regard as to where it had landed, but she knew she had shattered the glass as equally as the men in her life had shattered her heart.

The following morning as Amy got out of bed, the pit of her stomach was in knots. She felt ill and knew she could not continue on any longer like this. Her ship had sunk, and she knew she could get it back up to the surface if she pushed hard enough. After that, she just needed to stay afloat and keep out of wavy waters so she wouldn't go down again. She was the captain of her own ship, and she should have held on to the wheel a lot harder. But she didn't and let go. What she needed was to have someone else at the helm with her and stay on course. She knew who to ask. She hadn't forgotten about the broken glass that she left behind last night. It had to be cleaned up, and she made it her priority to do so before someone stepped on it.

With her legs crossed, Dr. Mackenzie sat across from Amy, focusing on every detail of her mannerisms. "So how have things been since I saw you last?"

"I'm not really sure where to begin."

"How about at the beginning. That would be a good place to start."

"I don't know exactly where the beginning is. I have been so out of touch with reality for a long time now. I don't even feel like me."

Dr. Mackenzie watched Amy fidget as she spoke. "That bad, huh? What else is happening?"

"I have problems sleeping at night so that when I am awake during the day, I am tired and have no energy to do things around the house. I am either on the couch or in my room lying down. I think it is more the solitude that I search for. I am so down that I cannot shake it."

"How is your diet, Amy? You are a lot thinner than I am used to seeing you."

"I eat much less than normal, and it takes some effort. Sometimes the food seems tasteless."

"So would you say that the ability to function and be yourself on a daily basis is affected by the way you are feeling?"

"Yes. I have less of an interest in being around people or doing anything. You know, going shopping, watching a movie, or even leaving the house."

"Amy, thinking back to how you were feeling before Nick left, would you say that you are feeling the same or worse?"

"Definitely worse. I have never felt this way before. At times I feel like I am in this dark place, and the longer I stay in it, the harder it is to get out. I have to refocus just to want to take a shower or get dressed. I am so afraid to go out in public because I feel like when people look at me, they know what is wrong. I think Paula hates me, and as for Aaron, well, he is not in my life right now."

"Why do you get the idea that Paula hates you?"

"Because I haven't been a very good mother lately. I've shirked on my duties, and she has every right to despise me. Heck, I would despise myself too if I were in her shoes."

"That is the way you perceive things at the moment because you are depressed. Tell me about Aaron."

Licking her lips, she put her head down. "He walked out of my life because I was a mess. He doesn't understand."

"Did you help him?"

"What?"

"Did you help him understand? Rather, did you tell him about your depression?"

"No. I never mentioned it to him or anyone else for that matter."

"Why not? Don't you think that if he had have known, he would have understood?"

"I don't know. I wanted to keep it a secret. I didn't want him to think there was something wrong with me, like I am going crazy or something."

"No, you're not. Amy, I am glad that you decided to come in and see me today although this visit was long overdue. When you get into a state such as this, you need to come and see me right away or seek other medical attention. When we spoke last year, I mentioned that you were suffering from depression, which is why I started you on medication. Your symptoms, however, have gotten worse; and when people just carry on like that, they think that life will never get better for them."

"Yes."

"Depression is a condition where chemical messages aren't being delivered correctly between our brain cells. With proper treatment, you will start to feel like yourself again. I would like to put you on a bit of a program, and it may be hard on you to try to stick with it, but it will help with the healing process. Try eating three meals a day, whether you just have a piece of fruit for lunch or breakfast. The other thing I would like you to do is to get at least an hour's exercise in every day, by either riding your bike if you have one or going for a walk. With the exercise and sleeping less during the day, you may find that you are sleeping much better at night. Do you think you could give this all a fair try?"

"Yes."

"We can also take a look at your medication, maybe try something else that may work better for you. Let me ask you a question. Do you like yourself at the moment?"

"No, not really."

"I am not surprised that you came back with that response. How do you feel about me setting up some counseling for you?"

"Maybe later. I think I have enough to work through at the moment."

"Amy, support groups are important, and you can find those within the people around you. Don't be afraid to use them by asking for help and guidance when you need it. Also, I think it would be a good idea to be honest with those around you if you want any relationships to work. You are going to have some good days and some very bad days, so hiding is just going to push people away from you because they don't understand. I would like to see you in my office once a week, just to see how you are doing. You'll make it through, Amy. Just give it some time."

As the elevator came to a stop, Amy waited for the doors to open. She would have rather taken the stairs so she didn't feel so claustrophobic, and she would have if it hadn't been for the heels she was wearing on her feet. They were not suitable for walking far distances. Her feet ached, and she swore she could feel the beginnings of a blister.

"Hi, Amy. What brings you to this part of town?"

"Oh, hi, Nancy. I was wondering if Aaron was in by any chance."

"He is, but let me see if he is free."

Amy looked at the pictures hanging on the wall while she waited. "Those paintings are abstract art. What you see is depicted through color, patterns, and shapes, making it harder to actually identify the real object or focus of the picture."

She did not hear him come up behind her. Without turning around, she continued with what she was doing. "They are somewhat puzzling but vibrant nonetheless."

"Yes. They are my favorite forms of art as it leaves you wondering what the artist is portraying. In case you didn't know, a picture always tells a story."

Pulling her eyes away, she turned and looked at him. "So what sort of story do these tell you?"

Putting his hands in his pants pockets, he glanced at them. "That I haven't figured out yet. If I come up with one though, I will tell it to you. Anyways, I know you didn't come here to talk about paintings. What can I do for you?"

"I won't take up too much of your time as I imagine you are quite busy."

"When am I not? However, there is nothing too pressing at the moment that can't wait."

"There are some things that I would like to say, so could we step into your office?"

"Sure." Ushering her inside, he shut the door and offered her a seat. "So what is on your mind?"

"I saw the doctor this morning. I also haven't been totally honest with you or myself for that matter."

Aaron waited for her to continue.

"I first saw the doctor about a year ago when Nick and I were still together, and I was started on medication for depression. Things were not that bad then; but I guess with Nick leaving, my father's death, and losing the baby, things got a lot worse. I know I should not have let it get so out of control, but I did."

"What made you finally decide to see the doctor?"

"I just couldn't do it anymore. I was sunk so deep into the sand. I couldn't move. I couldn't think straight. I was having a hard time just trying to survive."

He could tell by her body language that it wasn't easy for her to confide in him. "So what did she say?"

"Pardon?"

"Your doctor. What did she say?"

"Um, that I should have come in sooner to see her and that I can get better with proper treatment. She also made me realize I should have been honest with myself but more importantly honest with you."

"I am not all that up to date with depression because I have never been around anyone who suffered with it. Why did you lie to me, Amy?"

"I didn't exactly lie to you. I just chose not to tell you."

"It was lying. You knew what was wrong and how to fix the situation, but you made me believe you didn't know. That was a mistake on your part."

"Aaron, I admit it was wrong, and I am sorry."

"You have no idea, Amy. Our relationship was going in a direction that I didn't like and didn't want. So if you came here today with hopes of salvaging anything –"

"Aaron, please. I came here to try to make things right. I have missed you so much, and yes, I was hoping we could wipe the slate clean and go from there. Forgive me for saying so, Mr. Perfect, but I never thought you were the type to hold a grudge and give up so easily." Tears welled up in her eyes, and she dug through her purse to find a Kleenex. Pulling a handkerchief out of his coat pocket, he handed it to her.

"Thank you. I guess I should never have come here today. I'll just go now, and I won't bother you again."

Aaron knew his life was on the line, and he needed to think fast. She had no idea that since he had seen her again, he was remembering how she felt when they made love, and he had the strongest urge to kiss those succulent lips. She had caused him to have conflicting feelings, but the one thing he wasn't confused about was that he still wanted her. Her presence had weakened him to the core, and if he didn't get over his stubbornness, it would be harder for him once she walked out. As she started for the door, Aaron called out to her. Turning around, he was standing there with his hands at his sides, looking a bit flustered.

"Amy, you forgot something."

"I did? What?"

"This."

Pulling her into his arms, he crushed her mouth with his, making up for all the time they had been apart.

CHAPTER 9

ALL THAT LIT the room was the lamp sitting on the desk as her eyes focused on her fingers pressing the letters. She was neither very familiar with the keyboard, nor was she an experienced typist. It had taken a bit to get nearly one page of a letter completed. Hearing the doorbell, she got up from her desk and went to the door.

"Aaron! Come in."

"Hi, Amy."

Glancing at him, she noticed the smooth, clean-shaven face with his dark hair attractively styled and his blue eyes sparkling. They reminded her of water being touched by the sun. Glistening gems of the ocean.

"You are looking charming this evening. What brings you to this neck of the woods?"

"I thought I would stop by and see if the most beautiful woman I know would be up for a movie or a drink. My treat." Tossing back her hair, she smiled. "That is awfully sweet of you, and you couldn't have come by at a better time because Paula is spending the weekend with her dad. He has a new girlfriend and wanted the two of them to meet. Can't wait to hear all about it."

"Ah, and here I thought we may be on a time limit. Seems to me we have all night."

Reaching for her, he put his arms around her waist, drew her close, and nibbled on her ear.

Snuggled close to him, Amy giggled at the ticklish feeling that was going through her.

"Having you in my life is definitely worth it, but if you keep that up, we won't be going anywhere."

"Sorry, love. Guess I kind of lost track of things here. What would you like to do?"

Running her hands up Aaron's chest and then wrapping them around his neck, she thought for a moment.

"Hmm. I don't think I am up to seeing a movie, so how about a drink?"

"Sounds good to me. Do you have any place in particular in mind?"

"No. Surprise me."

"My pleasure. Ready to go?"

"In a moment. I just want to quickly change first and freshen up."

Watching her head up the stairs, Aaron paced with his hands in his pockets while he waited for her. He had to get himself together before he ravished her right then and there. Amy stood by her closet, quickly searching through the hangers of clothes. She hated that she didn't know where they were going and didn't have all night to go through her entire wardrobe. Settling on a pair of her finest jeans and a low-cut blouse, she put them on. Slipping on some shoes, she left the room. His mouth was dry. She looked very appealing. He was afraid to swallow, and for a mere second, he traced a finger along her jawline.

"I guess we should be going?"

Amy's expression never wavered. "We should."

He took her to a lounge, which was crowded with patrons, and the sounds of a piano played softly in the background amongst the high level of noise. Taking a table close by, Aaron pulled a chair out for Amy and then took a seat facing her. Deciding on a bottle of Chardonnay white wine, he motioned for the waiter and ordered.

"Would you like to dance?"

Surprised, she looked at him. "I must warn you before I accept that I have two left feet."

Chuckling, he slid back his chair and, getting up, held his hand out and escorted her to the floor. With one arm circled around her waist and the other holding her hand against his chest, he asked, "Are you familiar with this song?"

"Yes, I am. It is Celine Dion's 'My Heart Will Go On.' I have never heard it played solely on piano. It is breathtaking."

"So are you, my love. I have seen the movie *Titanic* more than once. Call me a sucker for romance. I can just envision you lying on the bed just as Rose did while I sketch the total beauty of your nakedness."

"Aaron, you are too much. I am truly shocked that you should think of me in such a state."

"Liar. I doubt your every word. I imagine you would love to pose for me just as much as you love the feel of my hands on your body."

"I had no idea that you are such an artist. Who shall I compare you to? Let's see. Van Gogh?"

He whispered in her ear, "My artistic abilities are not nearly that great. My talent is more like straight lines all connected. Everything looks like a broomstick. I dance better than I draw."

Laughing, Amy kissed his cheek. "I do believe that our song has ended."

"Indeed it has." Taking her arm, he led her back to their waiting drinks.

Picking up his wineglass, he took a sip and then looked at her, amused.

"You dance very well, love. I thought you told me you had two left feet?"

"I do. I haven't had a lot of experience on the dance floor. Believe me." With her eyes twinkling and a smile on her face, she continued. "It must have had everything to do with the man I was dancing with, don't you think?"

"I certainly cannot take all the credit. You are very svelte when you move.

"By the way, I wanted to ask how your mother is faring."

"She is doing great. She had the house repainted, which hasn't been done in years. Dad was sort of an old stickler when it came to changing things. He figured if there was nothing wrong with it, then leave it alone."

"Your parents each with a strong mind of their own. That must have worked well."

"Believe me, they butted heads many a time. Now, she has been looking at new decor." Finishing off her wine, she set her glass down and leaned slightly forward across the table, exposing some of her cleavage. Her eyes were glazed and sensual. "Listen, sailor, I was thinking we should go back to my place. What do you say?"

"Now?"

"Yes. Right now."

"Are you sure that is what you want? It's not that I don't want to make love to you. It's that we don't have to rush things."

"I want you, Aaron, and I don't see the need to delay the inevitable."

"I have a different idea then. How about we go back to *my* place instead."

"I'd like that. Let's get out of here."

His penthouse apartment was stunning and spacious. All the rooms had a window and access to a balcony. The bedroom was entirely masculine. It lacked ornaments, candles, and color; but it brought her closer to him in a sense. It was his world, his style. Moving his hand underneath her top, he caressed her breasts. Cupping her face with the other hand, he explored her mouth with his tongue. Amy moaned from the tingling sensation travelling through her body. Feeling her fingers on his zipper, he took her hand and pressed it against his manhood so she could feel the stiffness. Rubbing him gently, she could feel him throbbing beneath her fingers. Like an animal wanting to be set free, he growled. Releasing himself of his clothing, they moved slowly toward the bed, stretching their bodies out. If he had any qualms earlier about bedding her, he certainly had none now. Aaron was very detailed and professional in the way he kissed her neck, his mouth making its way down to her breast, circling and pulling at the nipple. She hadn't realized she had been holding her breath. Letting it out, Amy quivered beyond control when he went past her abdomen, brushing the soft mound of curls and stroking her most sacred spot. She was lost deep into the depths of erotism. "Oh, Aaron, I want you. Please don't stop."

"Oh god, Amy. What you do to me." Amy ran her hands through Aaron's hair. "Aaron, turn onto your back for me."

"Do with me what you will, my sweet." Shifting positions, she ran her lips down his body until she reached his swollen manhood and gently took it in her mouth. Moving slightly in rhythm, Aaron felt like he was about to explode from the arousing emotions and heat shooting through his body. "Amy, love. Come here. I want you so bad." Straddling him, he inserted himself deep inside her; and as she moved, he knew it was not going to take long to achieve climax. Leaning forward, Amy put her hands on Aaron's muscled shoulders and, finding his bottom lip, gently nibbled on it as he passionately whispered sweet words. It was at the same moment that he spilled his seed that Amy cried out. He could feel her contracting inside, and he knew there was nothing more bonding and fulfilling than the both of them simultaneously uniting. "I love you, Amy." With their bodies still joined, she whispered back into the dark. "I love you too."

It was extremely hot. She had called a cab and asked to be driven downtown. Rolling the window down, there was no breeze to aid the heat. She could feel the perspiration on her forehead. "Excuse me, sir, do you have air-conditioning at all?"

"Nope. I'm afraid it is broken, and the boss hasn't gotten around to fixing it yet."

"Wonderful. You must about die in this heat. How do you manage?"

"You get used to it, I guess. No sense in complaining about it to the boss, man. All he'd say is look for another job if you don't like it or fix it yourself. I sure ain't doin' that. Could be lookin' at big bucks there."

"Sounds like your boss needs his head rattled."

"Hah, lady, you got that right. Most of the workers is afraid of him." Thank goodness she didn't have all that far to go. Glancing at her watch, she knew Dee would be closing her shop soon for the day. Pulling up in front, Amy paid the driver with a sympathetic look. "Good luck with the air-conditioning."

"Thanks, lady. You have a good one now."

Dee came bustling through from the back. "Amy, what a pleasant surprise!" Holding out her arms, she hugged her affectionately, kissing the side of her cheek. "How have you been, my dear?"

"I certainly have my days, but other than that, things are going okay."

"Well, I am glad you stopped by. It has been awhile. I was starting to think you skipped town. You look like you could use something to drink. How about an ice-cold soda?"

"You don't know how wonderful that sounds. It is rather quiet in here. Has it been like that all day?"

"Pretty much, dear. The heat will drive the customers away. I mean, really, who wants to be out and about in this temperature? The older folk stay in trying to keep cool, and the rest head to the beach for the day."

"Ya, I suppose so. Do you close shop at all in the summer and take holidays for yourself, Dee?"

"I sometimes do, yes. I am not one for travelling so much now that I'm older. So tell me, things going well with you and Aaron?"

"We had a bit of a rough patch, but I think things are back to normal."

"Do you want to talk about it?"

"To make a long story short, I suffer from depression. I never did let on to Aaron, and it got out of control. So much so that I didn't do anything about it, and Aaron had enough and left."

"Oh my. That pretty much says it all."

"We didn't see each other for a few days. I tried to contact him, but he wouldn't take my calls. He needed time, I guess, to sort out his feelings. I know he was quite angry with me."

"I hope you have things patched up now?"

"Yes, but it was like starting from scratch all over again. All simple tiny steps to get to where we are now. After I finally had a reality check and saw my doctor, I went to his office hoping he would be there and see me."

"And was he?"

"Yes, and it ended better than it had started out to be. It was rough when he wasn't around, Dee. I was in love with him, and I thought I had lost him forever. I mean, I literally sabotaged things. Aaron got desperate and did the only thing he could do, which was leave. I don't think I gave him too many choices."

"Aw, honey, I know you have been through a lot, but don't blame yourself entirely. My sister suffered badly with depression, so I know how it goes. Although my brother-in-law knew what was wrong with her, he had a hard time dealing with it. I suppose mostly because he was ignorant about it all, so finally I got him all sorts of pamphlets and told him to start reading. Things were stressful for a time, but he took more of an active interest in trying to help her through it all. Their marriage survived, but sadly he passed away almost two years ago."

"I am sorry to hear that, Dee, but I am glad that things worked out for them. I missed Aaron so much, and the hardest thing was that I kept thinking he wasn't ever going to come back."

"But he did, didn't he?"

"Yes."

"Well then, don't worry about what 'was' and enjoy what you both have now and carry on. Funny thing about life, it has a way of sorting itself out."

Leaning over, Amy hugged Dee. "I am glad that I came by to visit as you always seem to know what to say."

"Well, I don't know all the answers, but it comes from experience and from the heart."

"Dee, you are such a good friend, and I truly appreciate you."

"Anytime, dear, anytime."

"I had better go now. I am going to pop over to the market for a couple of things and then head off home."

"Okay. Keep your chin up. You hear? And don't be a stranger."

"I won't. Bye, Dee."

"Good-bye, luv."

As Amy left the store, there was a slight skip to her step as she walked along the sidewalk.

Standing at the window in his sixth-floor office, Aaron stared out with his arms folded across his chest. His day had been pretty much wasted as his mind kept drifting to Amy. When he was away from her, especially at night, he wanted her beside him so that he could take her in his arms and make love to her. Just that thought aroused him. He was starting to think more along the lines of commitment, but he needed to be sure enough. Perhaps that trip to Hawaii he had mentioned earlier in the year would give him the opportunity to clear his head and help him sort his feelings out. Glancing at his watch, he was surprised to see that it was already past midafternoon. Coming to a decision, he sat down at his desk, picked up the phone, and dialed Amy's number, hoping she would pick up.

"Hello?"

"Hi, babe. It's me."

"Aaron. Where are you?"

"I am still at the office. I had something on my mind though that I wanted to talk over with you."

"Okay. I'm all ears."

"I was thinking that we should all take that trip to Hawaii. What do you say?"

"Wow. What brought that on?"

"Nothing really, except I didn't get anything accomplished today because I couldn't stop thinking about you. I thought it would be a great time for all of us to take some time off from the real world and have some fun."

"When were you thinking of taking this trip? There is only four weeks until Paula goes back to school."

"I know. I have to put a call into Beth yet, but I was thinking next weekend. That should be enough time to get all plans into place."

"It all sounds wonderful, but to tell you the truth, I cannot afford to take a trip like that right now. I am not working, remember?"

"I wasn't even thinking along those lines, so don't you even worry about it. If you and Paula would like to go, I'll take care of it."

"Oh, Aaron, I couldn't possibly –"

"Amy, forget it. Just pack your bags, and I'll worry about the rest. How does that sound?"

"Wonderful. Thank you so much for inviting us."

"The pleasure is all mine. Listen, I need to go and make a couple of phone calls and get this sorted out. I will be in touch with you later on."

"Talk to you soon."

"Bye, love."

The plane landed in Honolulu, Hawaii, and they were greeted with leis around their necks and taken by shuttle to the Outrigger Waikiki on the Beach. The hotel was truly luxurious, a beauty all in one place. Their oceanfront suite was done in rich natural woods, materials, and colors to reflect the island's style and heritage. Aaron and Amy chuckled as the two children ran around, deciding who was going to have what bed. "Aaron, this is absolutely wonderful. I have never seen anything like it."

"This hotel was built in 1967, and the waves have been surfed by Hawaiian royalty on this very beach. It also has the largest sandy bottom swimming area in Waikiki because the Apuakehau Stream happens to run right underneath the hotel and feeds into the ocean at the hotel's front." Walking over to the window, he looked out and called over his shoulder, "Hey, when you two are finished, come and check out the view." They rushed over to where Aaron was standing, and Paula's eyes widened up.

"Wow! Totally awesome."

Glancing her way, Aaron smiled. "That, my dear, is the Waikiki Beach; and from what I know, it stretches out nearly one and a half miles."

Adam looked at his dad. "Can we go swimming?"

"Whoa, slow down there, kiddo. First things first." Turning toward her, he touched the lei she was wearing.

"Do you know anything about the leis, Amy?"

"No. Not at all."

"Well, it is a symbol of Hawaii; and during the late 1800s, when visitors arrived by ship, they were greeted with aloha and floral leis. Then upon departing, if the visitor threw their lei into the ocean and it made its way to the beach, it meant that that person would someday return to the islands. The lei, I guess, has some legend of luck. So many leis would be seen off Diamond Head floating in the water as the ship left. Diamond Head, by the way, is the most famous volcanic crater in the world."

"Wow. What a beautiful story."

"Yes, it is. When the lei is given, it represents affection and is considered rude to remove it in front of the person who gave it. Anyways, my love, enough history for today."

"Do you know anything more about this Diamond Head? It sounds fascinating."

"It is actually. You can see it silhouetted if you look, just over there. Nineteenth-century sailors, British sailors to be exact, thought they had made a diamond discovery in the slopes of the crater, when in fact all they were, were shiny calcite crystals."

"Were these calcite crystals worth anything?"

"Nope. Totally worthless. Anyways, we can hike it if you like. I have been but wouldn't mind going again. There is a trail with a lot steps to climb, so bring with you all the energy you have. Also, if you bring a flashlight, we can go into the dark tunnels underground. You can see the old military bunkers too."

"You sure do know your stuff. How many times have you been to Hawaii, Aaron?"

"This is the fifth time. The first time I came here I loved it so much that I kept coming back. This is the hotel I stay in while I am here. I have explored some of the other islands such as Lanai, Maui, and Kauai. What do you say we get ourselves unpacked and then hit the beach for a bit."

It wasn't long before all four of them left the hotel with their swimsuits on, carrying towels and beach blankets. Keeping an eye on the kids while they splashed and swam, Aaron and Amy sat side by side on the white sand. Thinking how sexy she looked in her bikini, he leaned over and kissed her.

"What was that for?"

"Nothing. I was thinking though that I cannot wait to make love to you."

"You men are insatiable."

"We aren't."

"You are. What is the one thing that is always on your mind?"

With a look of mischief in his eyes, he grinned at her. "What else, making love. And I was thinking we could have a little fun right here on this beach at nighttime."

"See what I mean?"

"Talking about making love, I am getting a little hungry. What about you?"

"Aaron, we cannot just go off and make love right now with the kids."

Laughing, he put his arm around her shoulders.

"Take it easy, love. That thought never entered my mind. I was thinking more along the lines of food. More specifically, dinner."

Blushing, she picked up a handful of sand and let it slip through her fingers.

"Oh. I suppose the kids must be getting hungry too."

"I'll go round them up so that we can go back to the hotel and get changed for dinner. After that, I was thinking we could go for a walk and see some of the sites."

"That sounds great. I want to see as much as I can for the time we are here."

The first outing that was decided upon was at the Dole Plantation where they walked through the gardens and rode the narrated plantation train, learning the legacy of the fruit that symbolized hospitality. Never had they tasted pineapple so ripe and fresh. During the course of their stay, they toured Pearl Harbor and visited some of Oahu's neighboring islands; however, most of their time was spent relaxing on the beach, suntanning, swimming, and watching the talents of the local surfers. On the last evening, Aaron took Amy out for special dinner while Paula kept an eye on Adam back at the hotel room. The night was warm as they sat outside Chuck's Steak House, taking in the most amazing oceanfront view of Waikiki Beach while the sound of ukeleles played soft Hawaiian music. The sun had set over the horizon; and the colors of the night were a sky of stardust, rich in hues of red, yellow, and orange, which characterized the velvet cushion of the soft rolling waves. Palm trees added to the setting, one which was among two lovers. "Amy, let's go for a walk along the beach."

"Do you think we should check on the kids first?"

"I already took care of that when I visited the little boy's room. Everything is fine. Seems they are playing a game of snakes and ladders."

"Paula will try to keep Adam playing for hours as it is one of her favorite games. At least it gets me off the hook for a bit."

Removing her sandals, Aaron held her hand as they slowly strolled along the sand in total silence.

Coming to a stop suddenly, he turned to Amy and dropped tiny kisses along her face. When his lips finally reached hers, she wrapped her arms gracefully around his neck and turned the smolders into a blazing fire. When his mouth left hers, she could feel his breath against her skin.

"You know, I have had a wonderful time with you and Paula. I am glad you both came."

"So am I."

"I have enjoyed being with you and having you beside me when I wake up in the morning. I have been thinking a lot about us, Amy."

"Oh?"

"Yes. I had a few things on my mind before we came on this trip, and I needed this time to sort a few things out."

"And have you?"

"Yes, and I have finally come to a conclusion."

"Which is?"

Reaching for her hand, she could feel something being slipped onto her finger.

"Marry me, Amy."

She stood there for a moment speechless, which for him seemed like an eternity.

"Amy, say something."

"You're . . . you're asking me to marry you?"

"I am."

"I . . . I don't know what to say. I just never thought – this is so unexpected."

"For a start, how about yes. I love you, and I want you to be my wife."

"Are you positive this is what you want, Aaron? For me to be your wife?"

He searched her face. "I have never been more sure."

"I love you and yes."

"Yes?"

"Yes, as in yes . . . I will marry you."

"Tonight you have made me a very happy man." After letting out a loud whoop, he picked her up; and as they clung tightly to each other, they fell to the garden of white sand. It was as if the island was theirs alone as they took from each other like tomorrow would never happen. The only sound being was the song from the pearl-tipped waves as they majestically furled along the shore.

CHAPTER 10

THE FOLLOWING WEEKS were very busy and flew by very quickly. With the ending of summer came the finalization of Amy's divorce from Nick, and although she should have been elated, she felt like a whole era of her life had been erased. That chapter was now closed, like a book forever sealed into a vault, never to have the pages touched again; and for that she wept. What was so consoling to her was that she had a life with Aaron to look forward to and knew it was a journey worth taking, for she loved him enough. Playing with the 18k gold emerald engagement ring on her finger, Amy wandered to the bedroom window, noticing that the days were back to looking bleak and dull. She thought about the plans that were now in progress, for the wedding date was set for the last day in December, and they had been looking for a family home to buy. Walking over to her dresser, she picked up a set of black peacock pearl earrings that Aaron had bought her while in Hawaii and slipped them onto her ears. They were quite flawless and lustrous, deeply complimenting the fully lined two-piece grey wool suit she chose to wear to dinner tonight with Aaron and her mother. Just the three of them. Checking her makeup, she picked out a light shade of lipstick and ran it quickly over her lips. Her eyes, normally a rich hazel, had the tendency of changing color and were now looking somewhat of a smokey grey. Pleased with her appearance, she let out a sigh. Aaron had always told her how beautiful she was, and no one ever had to tell her how lucky she was to have him in her life because she already knew. With Aaron and Laina, there was an instant liking between the two, which was nothing of a surprise to her. Not wanting to keep the two of them waiting much longer, she quickly added a dab of perfume to her wrist and left the room.

The dining room was very breathtaking. Pillars stood in the center of the room; crystal chandeliers hung from the ceiling, sparkling like diamonds; and the bar was made up of frosted glass, mahogany wood, and gleaming brass. Heavy linens adorned the evenly spaced tables with fine cutlery and wineglasses. Amy had never seen anything so classy, and it appeared to be regarded with great favor by the extreme clientele. Aaron seemed very at ease and quite debonair looking in his attire while Laina sat quietly, twisting the long strand of pearls hanging around her neck. Passing each of the women a glass of champagne, he held his up. "I would like to propose a toast if I may." Looking over at Amy, he smiled. "To the woman who will soon do me the honor of becoming my wife. You are definitely indescribable, and to the lovely lady who gave birth to the woman I am deeply in love with." The glasses lightly came together, and each took a sip. Reaching across the table, Aaron grasped Amy's hand and gently held it while Laina smiled at the both of them, very satisfied with her daughter's choice of husband. He was a man of great values and structure, with a well-rounded sense of open-mindedness and loyalty. He was dependable as much as responsible. Dashing as much as spirited. So was her daughter, spirited.

"How are the wedding plans coming along?"

"Just fine, Mom. Aaron and I decided we were going to keep the whole affair as simple as possible."

Setting her glass down, Laina nodded her head. "You don't need all the expense and fiddle-faddle a second time."

Laughing, Amy squeezed Aaron's hand. "Well, Mom, I was thinking more along the lines of eliminating the stress that comes with the planning. I also want to remember and enjoy every minute of my wedding day, which is something that didn't happen when Nick and I married. With the wedding as huge as it was, I spent more time worrying about whether everything was going according to plan without any disappointments and disasters. Everything about that day was, and still is, pretty sketchy."

Aaron winked at Amy and lightly stroked her hand. "You will have no problem remembering our wedding night, love. That I can promise you."

Feeling the heat on her cheeks, she lowered her head. "Nice of you to make reference to that in front of my mother."

"Blushing becomes you, my dear."

Laina chuckled at the expression on her daughter's face. "I am quite aware of what goes on between a man and a woman. After all, I did have you, didn't I?" Amy's mind was interrupted by the sound of a man's voice through the microphone. "Ladies and gentlemen, could I please have your attention. I would like to thank all of you for joining us, and I have an announcement to make. We have a very special couple here this evening, who, in just a few short weeks, will be married. So as our band launches into song, please help me in congratulating them." As everyone applauded, the band played "When a Man Loves a Woman." Getting up, Aaron walked around to Amy and whispered in her ear, "I believe this song is for us, darling."

"Aaron, how did he know? You . . . you didn't –"

"Ah, but I did." As she was led to the dance floor, her eyes took in no one else but him; and as they danced, feeling the love they felt for each other, there was just the two of them.

Although the fuel gauge read less than a quarter of a tank, Beth decided not to stop and fill up right now as she was almost there. Her stomach was in knots, and she had rehearsed so many times in her mind what she was going to say to Aaron. Not that it mattered because it all amounted to the same thing. Pulling into the parking lot, she put the car in park and checked her appearance in the rearview mirror before turning off the ignition. Taking a deep breath, she entered the building and up to Aaron's office. Beth judged the woman sitting behind the desk to be in her early thirties.

"Hello, may I help you?"

"Ah, yes. My name is Beth, and I am here to see Aaron. He is expecting me."

"I will let him know you are here."

Aaron stared at Beth in disbelief. Since she had shown up, there had been nothing but displeasure and angry words between the two of them.

"I cannot believe that you would think I would consent to what you are asking. Are you out of your mind, Beth?"

"No, I am not. Besides, he does live with me, not you."

"That isn't the point here. If you want to move to Ohio with your boyfriend, then fine, but Adam stays."

"You are making this very difficult for me. I love Adam and want him with me. He's my son. But I also love Jake, and he is going to Ohio with or without me. I'd much rather it be with me."

"I see. Somehow I think you are forgetting that Adam is *our* son, and I'm telling you he is not going to live in Ohio. That is final. So the choice you make is entirely up to you." As his eyes narrowed, he continued. "If you decide to go, Adam will remain with me. The next set of words out of your mouth better not be in reference to taking him with you, because if they are, you know where the door is, and I hope it doesn't hit you too hard on the way out."

Beth stared at him with a hurt look in her eyes. "You know, Aaron, I have never known you to be so cold and callous, but maybe it is a side of you that was always there, but I never saw." Feeling a headache coming on, she rubbed her temple for a minute and, letting out a deep sigh, knew she had lost the race. She was out of laps to run and was in no way the victor. "All right, you win."

Crossing his arms, he stood silent for a moment. "This isn't a game of who wins, Beth. We are talking about a child's life, and taking him somewhere where he has to readjust is not fair to him. It is only going to cause Adam emotional upset. If he is with me, he will have more stability in his life. Think about that."

With tears in her eyes, she stood there with her hands in her coat pocket. "I am going to miss him."

"I am quite sure the feeling will be mutual. However, you can call as often as you wish, and I will be more than happy to fly him out to you for visits. By the way, does he know about this?"

"No, not yet. I thought it was best to wait until I had talked with you first and come to a decision. I am sure he will be quite happy to come and live with you though. I will bring him next weekend along with his things."

"Beth, I have a hard time believing you would give Adam up to me for a man in your life. I truly hope he is worth the sacrifice you are making."

She didn't respond. She couldn't. Turning around, she walked to the door; and as she put her hand on the knob, Aaron stopped her.

"I want you to take care. I don't hate you. In fact, I am concerned. If you need me, you know where I am."

Without saying a word, she opened the door, quietly closing it behind her, and walked the few feet across the reception area to the elevator. Crying softly, she pressed the button and had no idea that Aaron stood, watching her from behind with a look of sadness in his eyes as she left.

"Mom, it is absolutely gorgeous!" Paula was admiring the dress that Amy had just purchased for her wedding. Lifting the lid on a box, Amy pulled out a pair of shoes. "The saleswoman gave me such a good deal that I managed to get these as well. What do you think?"

"I love them. They are going to look so nice with the dress. Oh, I am so excited."

Laughing, Amy tucked the shoes back into the box and put the lid on. "By the way, I saw the perfect dress for you today, so I had it put on hold because there was only one left in that size. Tomorrow, if you like, you can go see it and try it on. What do you say?"

"I say, let's do it."

With the rains coming down as hard as they were, it did not have any effect on the mood of the three people looking inside a totally empty house that was for sale, looking to be bought by a lovely couple and lived in by a wonderful family. The house was absolutely beautiful, and both Amy and Aaron fell in love with it the instant they saw it. With nearly three thousand square feet, it was situated in a private setting off the main road with a paved loop driveway. The beautifully manicured and landscaped yard was huge, and as Aaron stood looking out the window, he already had visions of a play area for the kids with a swing set, sandbox, and tree house. He was brought out of his thoughts by the sound of Amy's voice and the feel of her arm around his waist. Looking at her, he could see her eyes dancing with excitement and knew this is where she would be content to live.

"So what do you think, Aaron? Do you like it?"

"I was just standing here imagining what it would be like to live here. However, I am not sure this is right for us. I mean . . . what do you think?" He could see total disappointment on her face as he waited for her to answer.

"I like it a lot, especially the outside; but if this isn't what you want, then I guess we just keep on looking." Removing her arm from around his waist, she turned to the realtor who was off discreetly in the distance, sitting on a stool. "Taryn, thank you so much for showing us this house, and although it is lovely, we are going to –"

"Buy the house, so you can consider it sold." Aaron walked up behind Amy and wrapped his arms around her waist and kissed the back of her neck. Twisting her face around to look at him, she stared into his eyes.

"But I thought we were going to pass on the house?"

Winking at Taryn, he smiled and felt like the cat that captured the elusive mouse. "That is where you are wrong, my sweet. I never said I didn't want it. You just assumed that I didn't."

"Oh, you!" Laughing, she kissed the tip of his nose.

"Matter of fact, out of all the homes we have looked at, I can't think of a better front door to carry my bride through and a nicer place to call home." With that, he kissed her softly.

December was definitely a month worth waiting for. Adam was now living with his father, and with the following days so full of activity, they flew by in a breeze. The morning of her wedding found Amy waking up early. Letting out a yawn, she stretched as a huge grin spread across her face. Reaching over, she lifted the phone off the bedside table, set it on the bed beside her, and lifted the receiver. On the other end, a sleepy male voice answered, unaware of the early hour that he was being awoken.

Smiling, Amy couldn't resist. "Happy wedding day!"

Chuckling, Aaron leaned over and picked up his watch. Looking at the time, he flopped back down and rubbed his eyes. "Same to you, my love. Do you have any idea what time it is, you little scamp?"

"Yes, but I won't be able to sleep another wink. I just wanted to call and say I love you."

"And I love you too. Are you up now?"

"No, still in bed, but I am getting up soon." The wedding was scheduled for two o'clock that afternoon, and although there was plenty of time, there was a lot to do. Replacing the receiver, and humming to herself, Amy bounced out of bed and headed down to wake up Paula and her mother.

Paula sat patiently while the hairdresser curled her hair in ringlets and then piled it high on her head, securing the hair with dainty little pearl pins, allowing a few tendrils to fall softly around her face. Slipping on the knee-length duchess satin dress of cornflower blue, it had a natural waistline with a thin satin tie at the waist. The bodice was done in embroidery and beading, and on her feet was a pair of delicate silver sandaled shoes. With tears in her eyes, Amy took in the finished look of her daughter and realized she had never seen her look so grown up and stunning. Giving Paula a hug, she pulled away and carefully dabbed her eyes with a tissue, hoping her mascara had not run.

Lauren, her maid of honor, glanced at the clock on the wall. "We need to get you dressed now. It is time."

With a feeling of nervousness, she let out a tiny laugh. "Yes, I suppose it is."

Everyone who needed to be there was already gathered and waiting in the flower-filled living room, except Lauren and the three generations of women standing in the bride's bedroom. Two of whom were watching as the dress was being slipped on.

Dressed in a three-piece black tuxedo with a white shirt, Aaron stood waiting for Amy with his best man, Tyson, at his side. Although he had the appearance of calmness about him, his palms were sweaty, and the anticipation was starting to get to him. The waiting. It wasn't as easy as he thought it would be. Glancing at his son, he put his hand on his shoulder and lightly squeezed it. It was at that moment that he knew she was entering the room because he felt her presence in the air. As he turned, their eyes met and locked, and he couldn't help but suck in his breath. His bride was absolutely picturesque as she slowly walked toward him. It was a vision he would never ever forget. Smiling, he held out his hand to her; and taking it, she smiled back at him. One that lit up her beautiful face and made him want to take her right then and there. As she was coming to stand beside him, he admired her dress of three-quarter-length ivory chiffon with scattered crystals and matching bolero jacket. Her hair hung loosely curled around her shoulders with a sprig of baby's breath entwined on the right side. In her hands, she carried sixteen red roses amongst baby's breath, each single rose signifying a month from the time they had met. Handing her bouquet over to Lauren, the two of them faced each other and took their vows, unaware of all those around them who had gathered to witness their joining as man and wife. Just as life is unpredictable, so was the weather, suddenly acknowledging itself. With the falling of tiny delicate snowflakes, he took her left hand in his and, sliding the wedding band onto her finger, promised to love her.

CHAPTER 11

THE RECEPTION THAT followed was kept in even tempo to the wedding. Lovely but unornamented. The bride and groom mingled amongst the guests, ensuring glasses stayed filled and the food was plenty, while Laina felt the need to arrange the wedding gifts in a more creative manner. Feeling a tap on his shoulder, Aaron turned around to find Tyson smiling like a Cheshire cat. "Come on, Aaron. Time for you to dance with your bride, don't you think?"

Amused, Aaron rested his eyes on Amy. "Well, my love, what do you say? Shall we dance?"

"I think we should."

Tyson walked to the center of the room and held up his hand. "Listen up, everyone. It is now time for the groom to have the first dance with his bride."

As the cheers and whistles could be heard around the room, the music started, with Amy and Aaron finding their way to the center of the room and into each other's arms. They were expressively euphoric. Kissing her cheek, he smiled at her. "Do you know what I am thinking right now at this very moment?"

"No. Tell me."

"I am thinking how very beautiful you look, and we should make a run for it so that I can make love to my new wife."

Laughing, she snuggled closer to him and whispered, "Just what would our guests think if we just up and disappeared?"

"By the way I see it, most of them will be inebriated, so if I were to slip away with my partner in crime, I doubt they would put out an APB."

"You don't say. As much as I want to partner with you, I don't think we should risk being caught and sentenced. Perhaps it would be wise to stay until everyone has departed."

Expressing his displeasure with a mere grunt, he found her lips and kissed her passionately, wishing the night would hurry up and end.

The honeymoon suite was done in modern elegance, with a four-poster bed and a bay window overlooking the countryside. Aaron pulled Amy close to him, not wanting to let go. God, how he loved her. There was no light in the room, except for the one candle burning, its flame flickering as the melted wax dripped into the copper holder. Though the room was not cold, a shiver ran through Amy's body as his fingers touched the back of her neck and gently feathered down her back. Pressing close with her face against the hair on his chest, she could feel his erection through his still-zipped pants. The sound of his heart beating vibrated strongly in her ear. She wanted him more than ever for the love and attraction was intense and profound. His head dropped down to find her already-parted lips enticing him to search her mouth with his tongue. Running her fingers through his dark hair, they kissed for a long time as he tasted the inner sweetness of her mouth, with no words between them except the soft moans and sighs. His eyes had the look of a storm ready to brew, and his body yearned with wanting. Scooping her up in his arms, he carried her over to the king-size bed; and as he undid his pants, Amy reached out for him. Lying behind her on his side, he kissed the back of her neck as he caressed her breasts, her nipples stiff and hard. "I can't wait to take you, my love," he whispered. As she turned over to lie on her back, Aaron parted her legs and moved down to her already-wet thighs, touching, tasting, and exploring. She was like the juice inside the fruit, waiting to be extracted and drank. He was greedy with thirst, and he couldn't consume enough to satisfy himself. Amy's body spasmed uncontrollably, and arching her back, she called out to him, almost pleading. "Tell me what you want, love." He both teased and excited her body, flicking the tip of his tongue over her clitoris. She was hopelessly lost and disoriented. Enveloped in fog. "Aaron . . . I want you to love me." Moving, Aaron lifted himself above her and knew she was ready for him. His shaft was throbbing and wet as he slid easily inside, her flesh tightly clasping his. Opening her legs a little more for him, he drove himself hard, wanting nothing more than to fulfill her craving. As he moved faster, she maintained a steady, flush rhythm underneath him. Aaron was panting hard and dripping in sweat. The room had a scent of muskiness in the air. He could hear her moan, but it was in the faded distance; and as he looked at her, he saw her eyes close and her head go back as she sought release. He could feel her, and driving himself like the force of a wind that didn't dare stop, he let himself go as he clung tightly and called out her name. With his strength entirely depleted, he collapsed on top of her. "I love you, Mrs. Daniels." As the last of the candle flickered and burned itself out, she whispered, "I love you too, Mr. Daniels. Happy New Year."

Aaron turned his head to look at his wife who lay sleeping beside him. Even in slumber, she was angelic. Brushing aside the hair on her face, he fixed the twisted sheets that bound him and, moving next to her, tenderly kissed her cheek, making his way down her neck. Shifting her position while she stretched, Aaron quickly scooped her into his arms and rolled onto his back so that she was poised on top of him. Tangling his fingers in her long tresses, he pulled her head down and teased her lips. "You have the softest lips," he murmured. She could feel his hardened manhood against her stomach and knew that he wanted her again. Deepening the kiss, she let out a slight whimper and was surprised when he suddenly rolled over and positioned himself atop her, easing himself within her. As her fingers gripped his muscled arms, she started moving with him, delighting in the physical bond. The promise of love. Grabbing her hips, he rode her hard like a stallion, pushing himself while she kept up the pace. Her breath came in short pants. Within her, he felt the spasms of release and moistness; and squeezing his eyes shut, he gave it one final thrust as he entered the throes of intense climax. Giving her one last quick kiss, he got out of bed and walked to the bathroom, shutting the door behind him. As she heard the sounds of the shower, she snuggled up underneath the covers with a feeling of contentment and drifted back to sleep.

The room had a brightness about it, the kind that came after a snowy winter's night. Adjusting her eyes, Amy crawled out of bed and drew back the thin curtains on the window. Everything looked like a winter fairy tale, with the ground evenly carpeted in snow and the long thick branches of the trees reaching out, never letting go of the white blankets that lay on them. Even still, with the minute flakes that fell from grey skies, it seemed to go on for eternity. Mesmerized, she slid the window open, peeking her head out, and deeply inhaled the air, which had a purity all of its own. She could see her breath in the crisp cold air as she slowly exhaled. Tilting her head, she listened, but not a sound could be heard. Just a serene quietness and beauty waiting to be touched. She could feel a pull all of its own reaching out to her. Beckoning and calling for her to come. Closing the window and locking it, she wrapped her arms around her chest, trying to ward off the chill that enveloped her. Allowing the robe to fall from her body, she slipped on her warm winter clothes and went in search of Aaron and the kids, finding them all gathered at the kitchen table. Looking up from the paper he was reading, Aaron was quite surprised to see his wife up and already dressed for the outdoors. He even noted the light spring in her step as she smiled.

"Good morning, everyone. Have you seen it outside? It is amazing. Anyone up to making angels in the snow?"

"Nope," came three responses from the table in unison.

Amy laughed at them as she slipped on her toque. "Aw, come on, you guys. How about some good old winter fun? Where is your sense of adventure?" The winks and nods amongst Aaron and the kids went unnoticed as she zipped up her boots, but the sound of the chairs being moved back made her look up. With his hands in his jean pockets, Aaron smiled at her, his eyes dancing with mischief. "We will be out shortly as soon as we get into our things."

She felt the thunk of being hit. Turning around, she saw another snowball in flight and just had enough time to step out of its pathway as it whizzed by her. It wasn't long before Aaron and the kids were standing in front of her with huge grins on their faces.

Amy stood with her arms crossed. "That really was not fair, you know, catching a girl unawares like that."

Pretending to look around then resting his eyes on Adam and Paula, he said, "I don't see a girl around, do you?"

"Nope," came the two responses.

She was about to open her mouth when the three of them started moving in closer, staring at her. With a sense of knowing what was to come, Amy continued to move backward, eyes huge and pleading. Like a pack of wolves, they stalked like she was their prey. In an instant, she found herself flat on her back with the largest of the pack sitting on her, arms pinned to the ground. He was strong, and as much as she tried to wriggle herself free, it was like being locked up solid. She couldn't even kick out with her legs, for two young cubs were lying across them. She had been completely overtaken. The sound of his voice was deep. "What do you say, guys? Think our catch of the day needs a good washing?"

Looking at him in horror, she tried to move.

"Oh, Aaron, you wouldn't –"

Leaning closer to her face, he smirked. "By golly, would you look at that. We caught ourselves a female here. I may be able to help this poor damsel in distress."

"Aaron, I warn you . . . I will do anything you ask if you let me go."

The silence as he pondered her words was like awaiting the verdict. She did not wish to endure the torture of this wolf in the snow.

Running his tongue over his mouth, he whispered, "This man yearns for this woman's kiss."

"This woman will happily oblige if your lips will seek mine, for I cannot move." His lips were cold when they sought hers, and it didn't take long before they burned from the heat of the kiss. The grip loosened on her arms, allowing her hands to move and quickly dig into the snow. Striking fast, sliding her hands underneath his clothes, cold touching skin, the only sound that could be heard was the sudden howl of the wolf.

Amy kept busy over the next few weeks. She wanted her life to be flawless and was determined to make it so. Adam had accepted the role she played in his life, and Aaron was attentive and undemanding. Dropping the overflowing laundry basket down on the couch, the phone rang. Picking it up, she was surprised to hear Dee's voice on the other end.

"How is married life treating you these days?"

"Oh, Dee, it has been sheer bliss."

"You sound very happy, dear. Are you all settled then into your new home?"

"Yes, pretty much, but it seemed like I was never going to get things organized and put away. This place is much larger than what Paula and I have been accustomed to."

"How is the rest of the family?"

"Terrific. Aaron cut back his work schedule a bit, so he is home by five now, and the two kids get along extremely well."

"That is so good to hear. How are things with you? You know, the depression and such."

"It's manageable. Having Aaron in my life has done wonders for the spirit. The doctor has even reduced my medication dosage, and hopefully by summer's end, I should be completely off. That is my focus anyways."

"You sound like you're in high spirits. There is a lotta life left in you yet, and it is worth living. Listen, the girl that I had hired gave her notice today for the end of next week. She is moving back to Australia to be with her family. Would you be interested in having your old job back?"

"You know, Dee, I wish I could; but in all honesty, my plate is pretty full right now. I have to say no."

"I understand. Thought I would give you first crack at it before I advertised the position."

"Hey, I appreciate your thinking of me. When you get a chance, come by for a visit."

"I plan on it. I want to check out your new digs. I have to go. Busy day today at the shop."

"All right, take care." Replacing the receiver, Amy folded the clothes and thought about her days at the shop with Dee.

As the water cascaded down Amy's back, she delighted in the feel of the warmth. She was in a particularly good mood this morning, humming away to herself. Shutting the water off, she opened the shower door and stepped out. The bathroom was like a sauna, the steam clouding the glass on the mirror, the walls built up with moisture. Opening the door, you could see the steam wafting through the air as it exited one room and entered another. Like the sky gently carrying the clouds. Being in no hurry as she dressed, she acted like one who had the world at her feet. Just as the bird in flight, with the freeness to go where he chose. No thought of time. Picking up her brush, she ran it through her hair and shivered as the wet strands made contact with her skin. With each stroke of the brush, she thought about her husband whose soft, gentle lips touched her body this morning, each kiss making love to her, never needing words. He stirred up her insides like a colony of bees being disturbed. The nectar it produced was sweet and excitable. Aaron's body executed strength, masculinity, prowess; and he had the ability to draw her to him like a source of power. Being brought out of her reverie by the sound of the doorbell, she put down her brush and went to answer it. The delivery man stood on the step, holding a huge bouquet of roses. Looking at the paper in his hand, he asked, "Are you Mrs. Daniels?"

"Yes. Yes, I am."

"These are for you." Handing them over, he nodded his head and walked away.

Closing the door, Amy pulled the card out and read it. "One delicate rose for each day since we married. When the petals fall, they will not wilt but remain as fresh and beautiful for as long as my love for you." Amy hadn't realized she had been crying until a single teardrop fell amidst the velvet petals. There it stayed. Gently laying them on the counter, she picked up the phone and dialed her husband at the office.

Adam and Paula came hurrying through the door after school, dropping their backpacks and slipping out of their shoes. They were both dressed in shorts as the weather was extremely warm for May. Amy was in the kitchen as the two of them raced in, both trying to talk to her at once. Looking at them, she smiled and raised her hands.

"Whoa. Hang on there a minute, you two. One at a time. Adam, you first."

Giving Amy the paper that was clutched in his hands, he waited while she read it.

"Why, Adam, this is wonderful. A top-class speller award."

Proudly beaming, he nodded. "I am the best speller in the whole class. My teacher said so."

Bending down, Amy gathered him in her arms and hugged him. "I am so proud of you, and I didn't know you were such a good speller. You top me on that one."

Pointing to the certificate, he asked, "Can I hang it on the fridge?"

Handing it back to him, she ruffled his hair. "Of course you can."

Looking at Paula, she smiled. "So, honey, what do you have to tell me?"

"Well, last week, the teacher gave us this huge math test. Everyone in the class was just freaking out about it. Today we got them back, and I got 98 percent. The highest in the class."

"Oh, Paula, that is absolutely astounding. Way to go! Math has always been one of your strong subjects. Sure wasn't mine when I was in school. I actually hated the subject."

"We weren't allowed to bring our tests home, but you can see it on parents' night."

"Oh. Which is when?"

"Next Tuesday evening. Seven o'clock."

As Amy was just about to respond, Paula disappeared from the kitchen as fast as she had entered it.

The tires screeched as the car turned into the driveway. Slamming the car door in anger, Aaron entered the house and, dropping his briefcase on the floor, headed to the den.

"What's wrong? The way you came tearing up the driveway and into the house, I thought the devil was after you." Standing by the window with a scotch in his hand, he turned to see his wife standing in the open doorway. He was so absorbed in his thoughts that he did not hear her enter.

"Come in and close the door."

Eyeing him, she did as he asked and stood still. His stance was tense, like a panther in a tree waiting to pounce at the first sign of movement. He was edgy, and she wasn't sure she wanted to stay and watch as the enemy was brought down. The room remained quiet except for the clinking of ice against the glass as Aaron finished the last of his drink. With a heavy thud, he deposited the glass onto the polished cherrywood desk that was once his father's. Amy waited for him to speak, and it was moments before he did.

"That son of a bitch. He better hope I don't get my hands on him."

"Who? What are you talking about?"

"Jake."

"Who in the world is Jake?"

"Beth's boyfriend."

"I don't understand. What does he have to do with this?"

"Everything. I got a call from Beth on my car phone just as I was on my way home. Seems Jake was out with his friends last night, painting the town red. Came home drunk as a skunk and beat the shit out of her."

"Good god! Poor Beth."

"She is now in the hospital with severe concussion and a broken rib, not to mention a broken nose and a few bruises here and there."

"That bad, huh? He sure took a round out of her."

"He is lucky I don't take a round out of him because he wouldn't get back up to see another day."

"Aaron, you don't mean that you'd kill him."

"Nope. Wouldn't go that far, but I'd have the satisfaction of beating the bastard to a pulp."

"Aaron, I feel sorry for Beth. I do, but she got herself into this relationship, and you are no longer responsible for her."

"We may be divorced, but she is my son's mother. Don't blame her for that."

"I'm not. All I am saying is don't take on her problems. Does she know what she is going to do?"

"Well, apparently Jake was arrested and spent the night in jail. Beth has asked that he not be allowed in to see her. I guess her mother is flying out to be with her."

"Is Beth planning on remaining in Ohio?"

"No. Coming back with her mom once she is fit for travel. Anyways, I have assured her Adam is happy here and can remain as long as he likes. He need not know about this incident."

"I agree. By the way, dinner is ready if you are hungry. The kids are washed up and watching TV."

"I'll be there in a moment. Amy, listen. I don't want Beth to come between us, and she won't. This will sort itself out. Thank you for being a part of my life."

Nodding, she left Aaron standing in the den and headed back to the kitchen.

The trees were in full bloom, and the grass had been freshly mowed. Standing at the cemetery, one couldn't have asked for a better day. The sky was a soft shade of blue for as far as the eye could see, with not a visible white cloud. For as long as it had been, Amy still missed her father, but she had been able to move on. Aaron was right. Time was the answer. Putting his arm around his wife, he watched as Adam kicked a stone about on the pathway. "You know, my love, I am so proud of the woman you have become. Our lives have been through tribulation and change, but I'd say we've come along way. You're a woman of real substance and strength, and there's a lot to be thankful for. I do believe we have your father's blessing as I can feel his smile from the warmth of the sun."

"I think so too, and I couldn't ask for a more blessed life than what I have been given. I love you, Aaron."

"I love you too."

The family closeness and love was a portrait one could only hope to have within their home as it had the discernment of unity and belonging. Amy rested her hand on her stomach and could feel the fluttering of new beginnings growing within her. This was knowledge that she had yet to share, but she knew with all her heart that nothing could be more fulfilling and complete. Thinking back to the moment when her and Aaron's lives collided, as much as she wanted to rid herself of another man, she knew that the course of events that finally bound them was a resistless force that could not be changed as it was their destiny to be one. Call it fortune or fate.

EPILOGUE

LYING RELAXED BUT exhausted in her hospital bed with newborn son, Robert, and daughter, Keaton, nestled in the crook of each arm, Amy had a hard time moving her gaze away from the two little miracles so pure and tiny. By some strong power, her head was being drawn toward the window where a bird was just landing on the ledge. With eyes fixed so intently, it was as if the sole purpose was hers; and for some reason, its being there felt appropriate. By any means, it was not invasive. Since the birth of the twins, Amy felt an ever-so-tranquil presence around her and, rather than being overshadowed by what wasn't to be, was content with what was. Repositioning a sleeping Robert, she lifted her arm and, placing her fingers on her lips, blew a kiss toward the window. Blinking its eyes, the bird stiffened only for an instant, displaying a regal and noble appearance, lifted both wings, and disappeared in flight.

Throughout the years to come, by signature, that bird kept an ongoing existence silently peering into the house that they had all come to love and call home. Observable and symbolic only to Amy, she sat in the rocking chair; and as the sun went down, the last significant image in her mind was the two of them silhouetted in flight against the night sky.

LaVergne, TN USA
23 October 2010
202000LV00001B/189/P